GUNFLOWER

Laura Jean McKay is the author of *The Animals in That Country* (Scribe, 2020) — winner of the Arthur C. Clarke Award, the Victorian Prize for Literature, and the ABIA Small Publishers Adult Book of the Year, and co-winner of the Aurealis Award for Best Science Fiction Novel. Laura is also the author of *Holiday in Cambodia* (Black Inc., 2013). She was awarded the NZSA Waitangi Day Literary Honours in 2022.

GUNFLOWER

stories

LAURA JEAN McKAY

SCRIBE

Melbourne • London

Scribe Publications
18–20 Edward St, Brunswick, Victoria 3056, Australia
2 John St, Clerkenwell, London, WC1N 2ES, United Kingdom
3754 Pleasant Ave, Suite 100, Minneapolis, Minnesota 55409, USA

Published by Scribe in Australia and the United Kingdom 2023
Published by Scribe in North America 2024

Typeset in Garamond by the publishers.

Printed and bound in the UK by CPI Group (UK) Ltd, Croydon CR0 4YY

Scribe is committed to the sustainable use of natural resources and the use of
paper products made responsibly from those resources.

This project has been assisted by the Australian Government through the
Australia Council, its arts funding and advisory body.

978 1 922585 94 3 (Australian edition)
978 1 915590 34 3 (UK edition)
978 1 957363 56 1 (US edition)
978 1 761385 39 1 (ebook)

Catalogue records for this book are available from the
National Library of Australia and the British Library.

scribepublications.com.au
scribepublications.co.uk
scribepublications.com

For Brea, Michelle, and Kelly.

And for Peter.

Ah, if life were not so fragile,
Death not so permanent.

ROSS McKAY, 1977

I gratefully acknowledge the Jagera People and Turrbal People of Meeanjin, and First Nations people of the Kulin Nation, the Larrakia Nation, and Gunaikurnai Country. Many of the stories in this collection were written or are set on traditional lands, where I have lived and continue to live as a coloniser and where sovereignty has never been ceded. I pay my deepest respect to Elders of these Countries and their connections to land, waters, and community, as well as to First Nations people across the continent.

I also wrote and set some of these stories in Aotearoa. I am deeply grateful to Rangitāne o Manawatū and Ngāti Hei Iwi. Ngā mihi nui.

birth

life

death

birth

CATS AT THE FIRE FRONT

My stepmother calls. She says, 'Jean, you don't know what you're missing.'

'Missing what, Annabelle?' She has woken me up. 'What?'

It's late morning, autumn. The light barely makes it through the clouds. I was up past midnight with Ed, doing the furs. There's scratch marks all over my hands, my fingers swollen purple.

'Life. You're not suited to this farm shit.'

'I'm well suited. *Well*.'

'You used to be a fighter. That's what I married in for.'

'You married Dad for me?' I try to sit up but that's not great, so I lie back again. 'That's a bit weird, isn't it?'

'Don't distract me. It's you I'm worried about. Drowning in this shit.'

My snort comes out high, sounds lonely. A nasal whistle will really put some people off, but not Annabelle.

'You've got nothing to fight for. Nothing to live —'

I laugh properly. Roberta toddles into the room and uses

her short wings to try to make it up to the bed. She misses, pecking the duvet in frustration until I haul her up with me. The chicken nestles between my massive stomach and the crook of my arm and starts a contented burr. If there were cigarettes, I would smoke one.

'Aren't you coming down tonight for my birthday?' I ask.

'Of course I'm coming. You know I am. I had a card all done up and I sent the link to everyone to sign.' There's a pause. I know she's sucking in smoke over there in Caballus Road. I know she's got a whole packet of menthol fresh. 'Your dress and my dress,' she breathes. 'We'll be like a pair of dolls. A pair of dolls from a birthday cake.'

'Dolls?'

'Yeah.'

'What's the problem, Annabelle?'

'The problem is now you're set to lose everything, and you won't stand up. Most people get married so they can fight.' Her lips smack as she smiles. 'That's why I got married.'

'I thought you got married because you had a crush on me. That's what you just —'

'Don't be crass. Your father didn't raise you to be crass. He raised you to be a little bruiser, in my opinion.'

'I'll knock you around a bit tonight if you like.'

'See, I would almost prefer that. I really would. Why even bother getting out of bed today?'

'I wouldn't if you hadn't called. I wouldn't be up 'til saucer time.'

'Saucer time? Saucer time, now?' Annabelle shrieks like a punch to the ear.

I gaze wistfully towards the bathroom, but Roberta is snoozing so cutely on my stomach and she's not always cuddly.

'We're not losing everything. Half the clowder, max. We'll be left with 120 cats, and they say if we can keep up production, we'll earn the rest back by the baby's first birthday.' There's a gulping sound on the other end. 'How much are you drinking anyway?' I ask.

'I'm not drinking anything. A wine or two at night. Maybe beer at lunch. Gin.' She trails off. I want to see if I can get my feet over the edge of the bed without upsetting Roberta. I can.

'I'm saying you've got to keep trying,' Annabelle goes on.

'For what?' I lie down again. Saucer time isn't for hours. Ed is out taking care of the cats. Roberta clucks in her sleep. I can rest, too.

'I can rest, too,' I tell Annabelle.

'You just don't get it, do you?'

'Nope.'

She's already hung up.

The swirl of fur and dust, and the smell of cat shit both acrid and sweet — the smell of life, for us. The felines appeal through the bars as I waddle through the caged aisles. Their pens are spotless — they like it that way — but they mew at me, shivering. Until last week we had the summer lights on, so they'd shed. Now it's back to winter to grow new pelt. Skinning is where it's at these days, but Ed was born to the shed: his parents did British longhair, now he does British longhair, and I do it, too. There's still a market for shed — in felt, catton, and yarn. We've had to make changes. Narrowed the cages to stop them licking our product away. Ed is up by the breeding pits at the other end of the barn, leaning on the pit rail and frowning into his phone.

'I've been messaging you,' I shout over the squeals of the kittens. He kisses my cheek with cracked lips.

'Look at this.' A cute Jersey/Friesian cross with bandy legs stumbles across his phone screen. 'Some bastard was planning to use her for milk.'

'God. Why do they do that?'

'Fetish or something. I've decided what I'm making for everyone tonight. Pony pizza.'

'We can't afford the cheese, Ed. Just do a stir fry.'

'We've still got that foxhound feta in the freezer. You'll love it. You'll both love it, won't you? Won't you?' Ed grins at my stomach.

'Have you heard from The Guy?'

He straightens. 'What Guy?'

'Come on, Ed.'

He runs a path through his hair with his big hand — follows the thinning line. 'He's just going to pop over. Tonight.'

'Pop over? In person?'

'IRL, babe. In real —'

'I know what it means. I said five o'clock to Dad and Annabelle. The Guy can just call. Email.'

'He wants to make things clear. Said it won't take long.'

One of the longhair gibs lets out a wrenching yowl. I need to urinate with a sudden intensity and clutch the edge of its cage. 'Let me talk to him.'

'It's my —'

'No, Ed, Annabelle's right. Someone has to stand up.'

Ed peers at me. 'You're taking advice from Annabelle now? *Annabelle* Annabelle?'

The gib wedges his muzzle through the gap and begins to lick my fingers tenderly with a raspy pink tongue. Cats can be like that.

Annabelle and Dad arrive early, glinting of battle. Some hour-long car rage that has taken them from the quarrel at hand right back to the start of their relationship and every grievance in between. It's impossible to tell who has won. While Dad bears a certain cowboy swagger under the weight of two fat boxes and a cooler bag, Annabelle is triumphant in a white Persian jumpsuit that looks set to cleave her in half. Ed takes the boxes. I kiss their freezing cheeks.

'How's my little girl?' Dad asks, his stumpy hand on my stomach.

'She's good. I'm good, too. Who are you talking to?'

'Your father talks to everyone, don't you, Martin?'

Somewhere in the flaky layered pastry of that marriage, this means something.

'Is that the dresses?' I lean against the door and nod at the white boxes. 'I won't be able to wear anything, you know, with this.'

Annabelle opens them right there on the dog hide in the hall and she's right, they are absolutely beautiful. Two tent dresses that shimmer and squirm like mermaids in a plastic sea. I reach to touch, expecting they'll be cool, but Annabelle grips my hand.

'You, darling, smell. Like cat.'

'I had a shower.'

'You smell like cat.'

We go upstairs to wash me and my hair again. Annabelle lets

me have a drag on a menthol that she ashes into the bathroom sink. When we come back down the stairs, resplendent and glittering, The Guy is sitting on our couch. Jeffries. Doesn't get up. Just sits there wearing a squashed, hairy face and a catweed suit like he's about to go on a hamster hunt.

'Good season for guineas?' I ask. Annabelle glances at Dad and smiles as affectionately as she ever does. Like, *well done. What a little bruiser*. Jeffries' face clouds. Just when I think I've lost him, and the farm, too, Dora decides to join the party. Jeffries breaks into a smile that's almost human. I should have called Dora in earlier: these men are all jumbuck boys. They won't give a pregnant woman and her adorable husband an inch but bring in a sheep and they're soft as kitten skin.

'Hello there. Hello.'

'Come on then, Dora.'

The sheep wags her woolly tail and gazes shyly at Jeffries. 'Merino, is she?'

'We paid for Merino but she has that lamby face, so we think her daddy might have been a bit East Friesian. Doesn't matter anyway' — I pat my bespangled belly — 'they're all good with kids.'

Ed shoots me a look. He's right: I'm scouting for sympathy.

'Who's a nice girl then? Who's a fluffy girl?' Jeffries settles back on the couch, his head against the rug Ed made last winter. Fur, fur. Our whole lives made of fur. And now this hairy Jeffries. 'We've got two Jacobs at home,' he says.

'Horns,' Dad puts in. 'Horny.'

'Yes, but no kids, no problem.'

'Ah.'

'Now.'

'Yes,' says Ed. 'We better make a start so we can get to our dinner. It's Jean's birthday tomorrow.'

Jeffries doesn't even twitch at this. Honestly, we'd be better off dressed as sheep.

By the time Jeffries leaves it's almost nine. Ed hasn't defrosted the foxhound or fried the pony. Me, Ed, Dad, and Roberta all slump in a line along the couch, while Annabelle and Dora troop up and down. Annabelle serves a nice red wine and some dachshund foie gras canapés that've gone soggy and brown. Dora is the only one of us that's happy, preferring groups and everyone still and silent. She rubs her face on our knees and lets Annabelle sit on the floor and pick burrs out of her wool. From there, Annabelle necks the rest of the wine and tries to fix everything.

'You'll just have to move in with us,' she says.

'No.'

'We've got three bedrooms. We'll build an extra bath. We —'

'No.'

'You can't stay here, Jean. This is a cat-fur farm and you're losing all your cats.'

'Did he say all of them?'

'He did.' Ed's smile comes out wonky.

'Who to? Who's the new place?'

'Hairline. They're big. Big scale.'

'Hairline. That's a really great name.'

'Isn't it?' says Annabelle.

'Cat Coats is good, too.'

'Thanks, Dad.' I reach over Ed to pat him on the knee. Dad catches my hand, holds it.

'I suppose you'll go into horses. Dogs,' he says, giving me a squeeze.

Ed shakes his head. 'We don't know milk or meat. All the equipment and everything except the outbuilding is set up for fur, hired from the company. Even the cats is hired from the company so —'

'Are,' says Annabelle.

'What?'

'Even the cats *are* hired from the company, and you're screwed.'

'Thanks. Thanks a lot, Annabelle. As far as cats go, we *are* screwed. We thought if we joined the big guys we'd get a better run, but we didn't. Our insurance covers the building and its contents and once the contents is gone —'

'You'll move in with us. Plenty of room for you and the baby.'

'What about Roberta? And Dora?'

The sheep eyes us, and we stare back at her long, flat face.

'It's dumb,' says Ed. His head is on my shoulder in the bed, voice muted against my milk-puffed breast. 'I was going to get that little poddy calf as a pet for the baby. They could grow up together. The poddy could stay in the nursery. They say the sound of the chewing helps babies sleep —'

'What's dumb about that?'

'Because it's what I feel worst about. Not losing the business or not being able to make mortgage or even having to move, but this little calf.'

'She's our future.'

'Was, right?'

I flex my shoulder, so he'll shift his head. 'We're still having the baby, Ed. That's still happening.'

He gives my boob a kiss and rolls off. I lose his slow breathing to other sounds. The cats in the barn. The house as the temperature plummets. Dad's snores that grind out of the spare room, up the receding carpet on the stairs and then come to a stop, leaving a gap in the world. A terrible quiet. I would worry into that silence as a kid. Now Annabelle worries. We usually find her on the couch when they stay here, the Alsatian rug across her body, hair like a bag over her face. But when I edge down the stairs to look, only Dora is there — sharp hooves scuffing up the dog-hide. The fridge whines from the kitchen. Roberta gives a warm brood from her perch, and it all feels lost already. Another snore from Dad rips through, dies again. I wait in the space the sound leaves, all our lives dependent on it. One snore and we lose everything, two and we stay. He snores again. Two snores. Two snores. We stay.

Another sound. Yowling that gets louder and doesn't stop. A light on in the cattery, illuminating the yard. I waddle over the freezing grass to check the schedule. Winter, still winter. It's supposed to be cold, dark, to let the clowder re-fur. The summer lights are blazing. It gets warmer as I move along the aisle, the fuzz caught up in it like asbestos rain, and the cats are quiet, slugged by heat. A figure down the end under the hot lights. My blood rises; the baby shuffles, too. It's Jeffries. Snooping around in the night. I tuck my hands under my

belly and get up a lumpy sort of a run, barrelling down the
aisle, ready to bawl him out. Squeaky, lopsided singing slows
my gait.

'Meow, meow, milk cat, have you any fur? Here are three
bags full, good sir!

One for the master,

One for the dame —'

Annabelle is cross-legged on the straw-strewn floor,
flannel nightdress hitched over her knees, a bunch of kittens
and the breeding dam on her lap. The kittens are getting up
a purr, stupid with milk. Even the big female is purring, her
grotesque teats laid out like half-filled water balloons on
Annabelle's thigh. A glass of dark liquor is nestled into the
straw.

'Put them back, Annabelle.'

She finishes the song. 'And one for the little boy who
lives down the lane.'

'Annabelle, hello? They're not declawed yet. You'll get an
infection.'

'From these things?' She lifts one of the sucklings by its
scruff. It cries out. The dam barely registers — we've got her
doped so she can relax, be fully productive. The kitten mews
harder, its bony mouth a battle against the hot air. At that
age they scarcely resemble the hairy, fattened livestock they'll
become. You can still see the wild in them — milk teeth
sharp, claws, too, limber bodies pouncing and crouching
within weeks. Soon, we'll wean them; in a few months we'll
de-canine and claw.

'Put them back, Annabelle.'

She drops the catling to her lap where it burrows with
the others to the teat. Annabelle's nightdress is fuchsia,

buttoned to her neck. Bits of grey wink through her loose hair. She looks the age she probably is.

'Have you ever seen one of these in the wild, Jeanie?'

'I've seen tigers on the ranches.'

'I mean a little cat, gone feral.'

'No, and nor have you.'

'In Australia a whole bunch of them got loose and they bred and bred. They're good breeders, but you know about that.'

The baby kicks me so hard in the kidney that I sink to the straw. Annabelle is encouraged.

'There's fires in Australia. Big ones. The cats worked out that if they waited at the fire fronts, all the little animals' — she drains her glass and wipes her mouth on her nightie sleeve — 'the bush rats, the small marsupials, would run from the flame to tiny tiger, monster paw.' In her lap, the kittens push the dam's teats, forcing the milk. 'The cats eat well that way. The sound of a eucalypt fire is like a bomb, like a freight train, and it scares the little animals. But the cats —'

'How can it be a bomb *and* a train? They're different sounds.'

'The thing is that cats are survivors, aren't they? More than that: they thrive.'

I frown at the female on Annabelle's lap, her breathing laboured against the weight of her teats; the cages around us packed with fat, patchy animals. Annabelle sees my expression.

'Maybe not them, but if they had their teeth and their claws, they'd be in it for a fight.'

The summer lights reach their zenith. Fur thickens the air. I try to get up, but the weight of my baby and breasts hold me down. I, too, am having trouble breathing.

'Annabelle.'

'Unbroken animals. Rewilded stock. Beasties, at best.' She's really gearing up now. 'Cats who ate through walls of captivity to the better wild —'

'Annabelle, I need your help here.'

She blinks, gathers the cats back into the pit, and extends a muscular hand. I get into a sort of crouch, rise up belly first to meet her. We sway like dance partners while I find my balance.

'I'll help you, sweetie,' she whispers in my ear.

'Thanks, I'm right now. Turn off the lights. Go to bed.'

'I'll sort it out.'

'You just have to make sure they're switched to winter. The cats need to' — I yawn, take in a lungful — 'to re-fur.'

I leave Annabelle in the golden light and go back to the house. The frigid night air can't shift the fug of tired that has settled over me. I stink like cat again. Haul off my nightie and undies at the back door and lurch naked through the house to crawl in beside Ed. He makes an appreciative sound; slips his hand around my belly, bracing us to his heat.

It's summer, I'm shedding. Thick, strong hair all over the bed — stumps of silk. Ed moves and I know he's gathering it, harvesting my fur. The cry I make is animal.

'Burning.'

My eyes fly open. A strange glow. Ed is rushing around the room, frantic. Downstairs, Roberta is going berserk.

'The summer lights,' I tell him. 'Annabelle put them on.'

'Don't you move,' he hollers. Trips over Dora who has

appeared in the doorway, wool lit up in the special light. I haul myself from the bed, edge past Ed and Dora and out to the stairwell where Roberta is trying to reach me by throwing herself against the walls. I catch her mid-flight and tuck her under my arm, feathers soft as angels against my flesh. It's darker downstairs, but Dad still pulls up short when he sees me — all distended gut and belly button, and pubes and boob, and Roberta peeking from my armpit.

'Holy hell.'

'Fetch me a wrap, Dad?'

He falls over himself to throw one of the sequined tent dresses over me. Takes Roberta and tosses her in the hutch. 'There's trucks or something outside.'

'It's just the summer lights.'

'It's the whole bloody shed.' Ed guns past, Dora behind him.

'Come on, Dad,' I yell, running with them.

Dad looks as though he's lost his reading glasses. 'Annabelle. Where's my Anna?'

The shed is tremendous with flames that take up a third of the structure, thickest towards the back at the breeding pits. Smoke rolls out from the open end. Dad and I guide each other around it. Ed is gone. Dora, too. Annabelle appears in a plume hefting a cage so cramped with cats it just seems like a box stuffed with fur. She sets it down beside dozens of others on the lawn. Mews peal over the flames. Dad lets go of me to run to her. I call for Ed. Stumble and weep past the orange heat to find him ineffectually dousing an edge with the high-pressure hose we use for cleaning.

'Look at this, Jeanie,' Dad calls me back. 'Anna has gone and saved all the stock.'

Annabelle winks at me, wipes her hands on her nightie. 'Insurance.' The roof collapses. I charge at her, thrusting my head and fists so they'll take the strike. Dad's face contorts. Annabelle reaches out like I'm coming in for a hug. The boom-rush of the fire like an exploding train. Just before impact, I hear another sound. A strange singing from the grass beyond the fire. It pulls me up. Again, the singing. Annabelle takes the chance to grab me, point me towards the cages. 'They're here, Jeanie. Even that big one.'

The breeding dam has a pen to herself. She raises her head to look confusedly down at her teats empty of kittens, then out past the roaring shed to the long grass. Something is singing out there, moving — I see it, too. Shapes that don't make sense outside on the farm, like underpants or computer monitors. I shrug Annabelle off my shoulders — my dress goes, too — and creep naked to the flickering verge of light. In the grasses: mirrored eyes, fireworks of fur, thick tails waving like snakes, mewing.

'Here now, come on,' I call. 'Come on, catlings. Hey, kittens.'

It's like they've become grass. White and striped fur now thin shadows, soft feet now air, prickly purrs now the cackle of the flames. Just me at the cold edge.

LESS

Shannon had completely forgotten to have children, and it was so embarrassing. Having them and leaving them somewhere would be less stupid. But she *had* remembered a gift for the third birthday party. A little ceramic ornament of a goat. The kid unwrapped it and threw it across the room. The statue bounced off the couch, broke a bit. The parents said, 'Oh, someone's tired!' Shannon wondered if the child would like to help her mend it and went to look for glue in the kitchen. A woman making SodaStream rolled her eyes. 'Kids. Who would have them? Which ones are yours?' Shannon replied that she had six at home but faltered when it came to their names. Billy, Lulu, Honesty, Fabric, Deedeet and ... The woman averted her eyes, shifted her body as if to protect her little ones, who were taking turns chewing the cushion of a stool. But Shannon was absent-minded, not dangerous. She wouldn't steal a baby! When she got home, she put the one-eared goat on her desk. How goats really look at you.

FLYING RODS

I am bitten late in the summer. Two sharp bites that come one after the other. It happens out at Tace and Erik's house in the hills, on a tamed lawn punctured by women in high heels and resealed by men in clean thongs — a party celebrating, as Dean says, the amazing fact that Tace and Erik are still together. I have been dodging Erik all night, but when I pull up the hem of my old sundress, he lurches over and crouches with Dean to examine the bitten skin of my upper thigh. We talk about whether it was caused by one insect, or two of them flying in tandem, like bombers. Whether they die after biting, like bees.

'How long do they live?' I ask Dean on the way home. The green dashboard clock is lit with 11:02. We've left the party early.

'*Someone should lick it,*' Dean says.

'Stop saying that.'

'Well, that's what Erik said, Kat. I think *he* wanted to lick it. Again.'

'He was so pissed. Did you see him with the vodka?'

'I think *he* wanted to lick it,' Dean says again as we reach the city.

I wake with a fever and try to shiver against Dean's comparatively cool body, but he moves away and eventually gets up to change the drenched sheets. I press my back to the cold bedroom wall until he gets back in the bed and his breathing is regular. I sit up next to him. My mind falls out of my head and splits on the clean sheets. It separates into clips, like a cut movie reel, and in the delirium I sort the thoughts into shining black squares of before, during, and after. My life in three flammable piles on my side of the bed. I pick up a square of before and hold it up to the streetlight coming through the gap in the curtains. The square is a still from a ten-hour clip of Erik and me almost two years ago in autumn, when Dean was away. The bed I'm in now. I have clothes on, but they're shoved up and down; Erik is naked.

I wake again to the paling darkness of pre-dawn. Dean is a distant mountain on the other side of the mattress. The glowing clock face reads 5:58 and I reach for a memory of whether that's the right time or not, then for the squares of memories from before now. And then I don't know what I'm feeling for. The horror of forgetting shivers through me until I fall into a sleep with no dreams. I wake again at 6:02. Dean is gone. I pat my way over the empty bed and when I reach the edge I fall and stumble towards the bathroom. The water in the bath mellows me and when it cools, I refill it. Outside it gets darker rather than lighter. Dean is a deep purple shape in the doorway.

'Breakfast?' I ask him.

'It's dinnertime. You slept all day. I tried to wake you, but you pulled the doona over your head. Are you ... do we need to talk about last night?'

'Last night?'

'Maybe this isn't a good time.' He leaves and brings back toast. I knock a bit of it off my plate, and we watch as it melts on contact with the hot water. 'How long you going to stay in there?' he asks.

'I'm not getting out now. The door is open.'

'You should go to the doctor. Or at least drink some water.'

'I've got water,' I tell him. 'The door is still open.'

'Erik called. To see how you were.'

'Who's Erik?'

Dean snorts and leaves. I spend some time flicking at the door with a towel until it swings closed. Then I sleep deeply, right there in the bath. I wake. The water is cold, and I refill it with difficulty. My hands shake. Everything is dim: red, yellow, green, and purple — there are no other colours.

I hear Dean's voice asking if there's a doctor who makes house calls. I hear the birds calling in the morning. The old doorknob rattles, and Dean comes in and tries to cover me with a towel. I push it off me, and it bubbles and sinks. A woman has followed Dean into the bathroom. She says she's a doctor and asks me how long I've been feeling this way.

'I don't know,' I answer, my chin submerged in the grimy water.

'She got a fever the night before last, and she won't get out of the bath. I was up all night refilling it with hot.' Dean turns to me. 'Do you remember?'

'I don't know.'

'To be honest,' says Dean to the doctor, 'I think it might be psychosomatic. We had a fight —'

'Could be. Katherine? I'd like you to describe your symptoms from when they started — that was two days ago?' the doctor asks. She has a tablet and stylus.

'I'm tired and I'm hungry,' I tell her.

'Yes, you would be, but if you could —'

'I'm not hot.'

She glances at Dean, then crouches and hunches over what looks like a tool kit. She gets a needle out and bites me with it, drawing the blood into the hollow finger and keeping it there.

When it's dark, Dean tries to coax me out of the water by holding a plate of spaghetti just out of my reach, but in the end we argue, and he plonks the plate next to me on the ceramic edge. It overturns and the red sauce and yellow pasta loosen their greasy grip and separate in clumps and ribbons through the water.

'Oh, babe, I didn't mean to ...' Dean stops. I am ducked water-level to eat my way through the mess, my mouth open and sucking, revolted and ravenous at once. Dean retches. I eat.

Dean is talking loudly on the phone outside the bathroom door. He says, 'Well, that's how it is, Erik. Go take care of your own girlfriend,' and then his voice is an inarticulate low buzzing that lulls me to sleep. It's just light when I open my eyes and get out of the bath. Try to flick the cold beef mince and tomato and bits of pasta from my skin, but the skin comes away, too. It peels in damp, hairy flakes from the top of my head. Then there is a hole. I squirm and pull until what has been my outside flops like a wet paper bag to the tiles. I kick myself free of it. Underneath there is another skin, raw and translucent. I find my way to the bed in the early light and creep under the doona beside Dean. He turns to me, wrapping his big arms around my slippery frame.

'Your fever's gone?' he asks without opening his eyes. 'You smell clean.' I burrow down and stay there in the aching, almost sexual clutch of sleep.

He's trying to get through the barrier of doona over my head. His voice is muffled, but loud.

'... know that jealousy can be hard for you to understand,' he is saying. I press the covers closer. 'But Erik was really coming on to you the other night and you didn't seem to mind. At all. That's what I feel. Felt! I meant felt. But I think it's making you sick and so I wanted to say I'm sorry. I trust you. I didn't, but that was ages ago. Now I do. I'm going to work and tonight I'm going to cook you dinner. What would you like most? Anyway, there's some muesli here now.'

'Now,' I repeat. Something I can grasp. I wrap my mouth around the word and hold it.

'Yeah, right here. On the dresser,' he says, then turns.

I part the doona to let in the bright yellow light and focus my eyes on the muesli.

It is there. The muesli is there. The muesli is there. The muesli is there. The muesli is gone. I can hear noises — metal clanging and water — through the door. It's dark. I push the doona off my head. The room is dark. I push the final slippery layer from my body and I'm free. Wet. Open the window by sticking the bottom of my foot to it. Pull. The foot comes away from the glass with a *shuck*. A wind blows in. I dry. The long, thin folds at my back dry. My tongue is a tube that curls out from my mouth. It doesn't dry.

I am perched on the windowsill when Dean opens the door. He turns on the light and I fling myself towards it. The folds at my back grow and spread and I reach it too fast. Glass showers down and there is darkness. But I can smell Dean. He makes a sound; a giant angry sound and smell comes from him. He thumps around in the dark. The folds expand again.

He yells, 'Kaaaaaaaaat getin'eeeeere', and swipes at me with a hand. He is slow. I can feel the heat of his motion as he makes it. I step aside though the air towards the window. And I smell the blood. Not Dean's blood, though there *is* that: a familiar metal. I can smell more blood, other blood, new blood. Out there. Untasted. Big blood and small. Blood in the trees and blood in the yards. Blood at a time different from now. A time I can get to. And the folds rise on the air and I go for it.

COME AND SEE IT ALL THE WAY FROM TOWN

Always rocks, just rocks. Random through the mid-paddock and hard to get to over the ridge. Dad stared up that rocky hill all day. The way they cropped up at angles and seemed to shift. Dad hadn't been in the top paddocks since he did his hip. Stayed on the porch with his binoculars, his spotlight at night, muttering at us to keep our voices down.

'It's weird.' Sam followed the light with their eyes, through the sheep paddock to the top of the hill.

'Don't worry about Dad,' I said. 'He just likes the quiet.'

'The rocks, I mean. There's an edge.'

'A stolen edge.'

'He'll hear you.'

Okay to steal land, apparently, not okay to say it. I hissed about colonisation, but Sam kept their gaze fixed on the paddock.

'Last time I was up there I heard voices,' they said. 'Not outside my head. Strange thoughts.'

'Maybe go up there *before* you check your crops next time.'

Sam wouldn't go on the quad bike with me after that, not for nothing.

Dusk time. Lonely time. I howled over the ridge, wanting Nugget to howl with me. The dog just looked very sad about the howling. Sun lit up the rocky side — that orange way — and I tipped the quad over the edge, rumbling down: golden-green with dark grey lumps sticking out of it. The rocks bigger there, trees and gorse sparse. The Waiau Uwha sparkling in the valley.

'We lost you here, eh — you were just a little pup,' I told Nugget. 'Didn't we? Didn't we?'

The dog toured the base of one of the upcrops where the dirt had been disturbed — like a giant mushroom had pushed through, except the mushroom was a cloudy hunk of granite. Speckled up close, like skylark eggs. Nugget came around the other side sniffing at the base. Then he said something.

'Hey?' I turned my gaze on him; I always was convinced there was more to that mutt than terrier.

Back down the hill I told Sam that Nugget could suddenly talk. I didn't say I'd also seen Sam in the valley, torchlight flashing around. Not very stealth.

Sam grinned at me, red-eyed, from the couch. Said, 'Of course he can', and started singing 'On Top of Old Smoky' until Nugget reluctantly wrinkled his lips, wailed along, too.

'But I heard Nugget say *what's up?*' I yelled over them.

'What's up with you? What about you?' Sam jostled Nugget's ears until the dog moved away.

'Actually, he just said *what*.'

Sam squinted at me. Got up and shut the door because Dad was out on the porch with his lights and notebook — a spotter, was Dad.

'You think Nugget said it?'

'Well, it's not like I saw his lips move or anything, but —'

'For me it was *blimmin*.'

'Like old-fashioned swearing? Nugget!'

Sam shook their head. 'Nugget wasn't even there that time.'

We wanted to camp up on the hill. Sam did a survival course in Ōtautahi last autumn that I was apparently too young for, so they knew how to pack a tent, a mat, and cooker, and the best food like cans and things. How to replace the wool blankets with camphor-smelling sleeping bags. Dad nodded approvingly from his chair. The sun was doing late-afternoon things so he didn't need a spotlight for a direct view to the rocky top. 'Take lamps. Lots of lamps.'

I said 'Got it!' and pushed Sam out of the way. I was going to drive the damn quad, at least.

'It's not a competition,' Sam said, climbing on the back with extra torches and headlamps. I whistled. Nugget pretended not to hear me. But when I started the quad, the dog jumped up and settled next to Sam.

Sam yelled that I should I go the goat track because of all the gear. I took the lip. Sam swore and clung on when we tilted over the top but then got to see how great a spot it was.

I switched off the bike. The voices were immediate.

'Nugget!'

Sam shushed me. The seat was so comfortably worn with Dad's bum dents I didn't want to move. Sam seemed content on the back under the gear, too. Wind hummed around us. Nugget started digging the base of the nearest rock. Sam edged off the bike to where Nugget was muttering away.

'That dog's been pretending he can't talk this whole time,' I called. But Sam pressed close to the rock.

'Up.'

I looked up. The sky low and pink.

'I mean. That was the word,' Sam said.

'What?'

'Up. The rock said *turn it up.*'

'The *rock* said *turn it up?*'

Sam nodded, listening still. I climbed off the quad and wriggled into the small ditch Nugget had made, face against the stone — scratchy, freezing. My ear cold and my steadying hand.

Sam knew how to make a fire and had brought stale cinnamon scrolls from the bakery they worked at in Waiau. Toasted, the icing melted and the sweet bread was lovely, burnt. Nugget liked it, too. We didn't talk. We collected rock words like we once collected river stones. From the house verandah came a series of flashes: Dad with the spotlight. Sam had learned some morse code in the survival course.

'What's it say?'

'Nothing. It doesn't even make sense.'

Still, we flashed back, longer and longer with the lights, until Dad was either satisfied or fell asleep at the switch.

•

Sam could still make out the words over the quad engine as I wound down the morning hill.

'*What*,' Sam shouted from the back. '*Up*.'

Even in the house, where Dad had made toast, we could hear it. We took the peanut butter and plates out to the porch.

'Go on,' Sam whispered, taking a big bite.

'You tell him,' I hissed back. Sam pointed at their mouth. Full. Impossible to talk.

'Shithead,' I said.

'Excuse me now?' Dad heard that.

'But Dad, the rocks are saying *blimmin'* and —'

'The rocks aren't saying *blimmin*",' said Dad.

'It's not swearing if Sam heard it, too …' I waited for Sam to tell me I was being a whiny bitch, but Sam looked stunned, like the possums we catch in the torchlight. Dad up and left. Finally done with us, I thought. He came back again with two old exercise books, some pens.

'Never thought you two would be still long enough. Well, you're in for it now.'

'We don't have homework,' Sam told him, giving me a Dad's-losing-it look. 'It's holidays.' Another voice. We all heard it and looked up the hill, dark against the brightening sky. Dad motioned Sam to write the rock words in their book, then made corrections. 'Not *what*, but *watt*. Not *blimmin'* but *lumen*. They're after our light. They reckon there's light — electricity — coming from our bodies and they're asking about it. Took me ages to understand that. At first the words were in te reo — but I don't know much about that.' He coughed and hid his face, adjusted his glasses, turned the spotlight on again. 'Now they've switched to English. I'm showing them a stronger light here. They're not much keen on it though.'

'How long have you been talking to them, Dad?'

'Since your mum. She's the one told me about it. Said they've been doing it forever. I didn't listen to her either.'

'Mum was ages ago.' We all went silent thinking about her in our separate ways. How she went around the place with so much energy, so bright. 'Well, what else have they been saying?'

'That the Iwi who lived here before us were better at sharing.'

Dad made us wait until night, and then it took ages to get him up and settled on the quad.

'You drive,' I told Sam, but they gave me a little push towards the wheel.

'You're better at it.'

I edged up there slowly, the quad light picking up every pothole. I was sure we'd lose Dad, but every time I glanced back, he was there on the rear seat with Nugget on his knee and Sam coming up behind on the motor bike. When I got to the lip, he told me to turn off the quad beam, so we tipped over into darkness — broad shapes of the rocks below. We all heard the word — as though someone had flicked a switch — but Sam called it first.

'*Light.*'

THOSE LAST DAYS OF SUMMER

That summer stretched yearlong, and we were always giving birth. We tried to make a game of it at first — taking turns in the narrow cells and pitching our cries like songs — but towards the end we were either just fat or skin. The cells formed a long hall, lit sixteen hours a day and always the same: a fearsome golden light coming from the roof; particles of skin floating through the air, in our throats, our faces; the sisters above us and the sisters below. We were all born to the cell and none of us, not our mothers or their mothers before that, really knew if there was anything but the slanting cage floor, our cellmates, the heat.

One of us had heard stories though. Said there was something more than standing and death.

What is it? we asked her.

Winter, she said.

And what else?

Darkness.

One of us had seen her sister die, two cells over. Sensed the familiar life coming to an end and it gave her such a shock her toes clenched over the bars of the floor. They couldn't get her loose. One thought of us all as sisters and rubbed her raw skin against the bleeding cage when another passed away. The guards would bring in someone new, and after a while she'd forget and call her sister, too.

Some of us didn't care, were beyond caring. We felt the rage of the endless day beat like wings that we bit and scratched at. When she fell, we stood on her, flattening her head into the bruising bars. When we gave birth, it was over her body, even though she'd passed days before. We had our teeth removed and our arms made useless, so all we could do was stand and eat slop with our faces. We stood the long day round. Our bodies grew fat and our legs weak and we collapsed on each other. We gave birth over and over again.

In the last days, the giddy, heady urge to birth slowed and then stopped and we shed hair instead. It fell down through the top cells and covered those below. To punish us they stopped the food and turned out the lights and we were plunged into winter. During that time we told each other things. One said the children we made were sent to war in three armies — the 600, 700, or 800 divisions — depending on their size. There were rumours of special units called roasters or broilers. None of them ever returned.

We're lucky to see the long day, she said, and we stood straighter, those that could, and appreciated our little space, and our warm faces and feet, and the feel of another's body up against ours.

Others said, no, the children were taken and raised as guards.

If they're guards, then why don't they help us? we asked. We could just make them out through the dim. Watched as they moved past on legs like the bars of a giant cage, checking for children. We wondered if they were our sons. We starved that winter, some died, and then finally someone gave birth and set us all off again.

The lights were turned on and the summer regained and those that had survived were rewarded with food. But we were different. One of us edged forward to eat and heard her brittle legs tremble and crack. She lay on the bars with sisters below and sisters above and called out. The din of us was terrific. We all spoke at once, in small sharp phrases:

She ate more than me.

She stepped on me and said sorry.

She's too old to have children.

She laughs when I do.

She lay there and heard our voices flying over her like a great fleet of cages. One of us fell on her and the nothing weight of her raw skin pressed until there wasn't much breath left. But she was still alive.

A guard came and opened the cell with his cage hands and grabbed her by the legs. She was carried upside down along the hall. As she passed, we called out:

Don't go, don't go; go, go, go.

We were never sure. The guard carried her beyond the lights and dusk came suddenly, then it was pitch black. She was thrown into it and for a moment she was flying. She stretched her useless arms for the first time and caught the air; then she came down. Her landing was sharp and wet.

She smelled the sweet smell of herself rotting over and over again. She realised that she was lying on broken bones and there was nothing, nothing! Between standing and death. There was no mother, no guards, no sisters, no cells, no skin, no food, no words, no birth — just the light and then the darkness. It fell all over her and sucked her back from life.

The summer just starts again, she told us.

She wanted us to know what that was like, to be pulled back into the womb. Like all this time she'd been something spilled and now every cell found the other, reminisced, reformed. She wondered if, when she was born, it would be as a 600 or 800, or even a broiler, whether it would be the same life she'd just lived, to the same mother, or would she be a guard, or something other? But she asked these questions very quietly, and from far away, so we couldn't hear her. The guards had brought someone new to the cell and we were already calling that one sister. Far away in the darkness she felt herself becoming small. Encased in warm weather. Liquefied. The heartbeat of home.

LIGHTNING MAN

I don't know where they find them. They're always in the dirt, licking things clean, and now it's on their noses, in the little one's ear. He's so hungry, like his brothers, but doesn't know where to stick things. Soon they'll come to me. It is a hard choice then — whether to take a lick of a lolly that's been on someone's tongue and in the dirt, or to shake my head and see their faces fall. They're like cats bringing the dead and the dropped and the sorry home. They take so much pride in what they do I almost admire the lengths they'll go to lick or pick the scum off a thing so that their first taste is a good one. I suppose they enjoy the process. Like Jo enjoys rolling his own cigarettes, and I enjoy the sun.

We have seats to the side of the arena. A little lean and there is the cavernous tunnel where the show will come out. The little one cranes so far over the edge to see the dark entrance that it seems that only his thin knees keep him in. My eldest has a careful hand on the little one's shirt though. I stop myself from counting each restitched stitch — wondering if the fabric will hold. Beside me sits the girl. She is clasped and ordered and most certainly not one of my own. She has gone from good home to good home, finally ending here, and she's already explained that the seats halfway around the ring would offer the best views of the show. When the boys come to climb on me, they circle her like they do the single plate and teacup that's left of our china. She is the cleanest thing they've ever brought home and has somehow remained so. Only the little one reaches for the curls on her head but snatches his sticky hand back, as if its blondeness would burn him. The girl sits and stares ahead during this ritual. She's a strange light in our flame-headed household. I can understand the little one's fascination. I would also like to touch something that wasn't boy and stitched.

It only takes a look from me to stop them from running to the top of the tunnel again. They're sensitive as the sky and they watch the slight tip of Jo's head and my glances with animal perception. I don't mind that they run or scrounge around. I don't begrudge them a lick of the dirt off their lollies so long as they all get some. But their leaning over the tunnel reminds me that I'm half-starved with worry. That I'd be hanging over there myself if it weren't for the nerves and for the girl sitting there so drawn and still. What does she think of me? But people who are bothered by others' opinions are people with time and money to spare, as Jo would say. With our packing and unpacking, over and over, our darning and baking and stirring the porridge in the morning and spreading the fat over the bread at night, who has time for worry? Beside us, the girl with folded hands is as penetrating as, and cleaner than, the great tent lights that shine down above the ring.

•

Jo and I had a tilt of the bottle each before we left — we do for a celebration or to give us luck. Jo laughed and said that's why we have to keep moving on, so that we can have another tipple. He goes out to be with wild animals with the confidence of whiskey warming his insides. It doesn't bother the boys, who run here and there around the chairs while we sit at the board that is the table and pass the bottle. But the girl watches our reflection through the crack of the mirror as she twists and spins her hair. Jo couldn't see — or feel through his merry back — the weight of her eyes through the glass. But that blue cut me, and I knew, then, what the neighbours thought: that we would never rise up out of the dirt that made us, that we were only fit to lick things clean, that we would be very lucky if the show were to take us and our bony breed.

The little one feels my body tense beneath him and swivels his head around from my lap. The others feel it, too. I see it pass on like a shiver between them as though they were all still lying one by one in my womb. But little one mistakes my worry and extends his grimy hand. All the rest stare with bleak eyes from the girl to me.

'Want some?' he lisps. The lolly drips in sticky clumps over his fist and he holds the wooden stick tightly. I shake my head, cheeks lifted to soften it. All around us the tent fills slowly, with people edging past and watching for the numbers on the seats and children dressed in froth and laces and, thankfully, a huge space around us — the designated seats for me and my own and for the families of the other workers. Little turns his brown eyes to the girl. 'Want some?'

The girl breathes out her nose. I wonder will the lolly drip on the clothes she has brought with her from the good homes? I can see, from the frippery of those sitting midway round the circle, that though her things aren't quite the fashion, they probably were, once.

They want to know where Jo is; you can see from their eyes and their straying over to the tunnel. Bending in and out like ducks on water. If I get the job, said Jo last night, we'll have a painted van of our own and one pulled behind for the little ones. Oh, I wouldn't want to be without them, I told him, distressed. That's the thing though, he leaned himself up on one fine elbow and smiled into me. I admired his moustache, long and black and twirled like a ringmaster. They go so slow, he explained, that you can hop right out of your van while it's moving and check on the little ones or play with them or give them dinner. They can run alongside and tease the lions or pat the elephant's legs, and when they get tired you can lift them up and pop them back in their wagon. I laughed into his armpit. Couldn't one of them be left behind? I muffled. A neighbour once told me that a man's sweat calms a woman's hysterics. My heart has beat strangely since Jo's news. I dug my nose in deeper and Jo rubbed his moustache over my ear. Have you ever known them to be more than a foot away? he asked, and as I shook my head, his shoulder quaked with me.

The air in the tent is filled with dust and people. Caged excitement. All of us, fine and small and huge and bedraggled, glancing sidelong into the ring while pretending to talk to one another. My boys have found their proper seats, feeling that something is about to start. Only the little one tries to engage the girl in conversation.

'That boy got a ball,' he tells her, and my heart hurts. The boy with the ball pushes it up in the air and then drops it. A man fetches it and wipes the dust off before giving it back. I pull the little one closer on my lap and begin to work on his hand with the edge of my skirt. 'That where the animal and the big dog and Pa come out,' he says and points across her to the tunnel with his still-dirty hand. The girl's head shifts slightly to acknowledge this. The curls sway and bump her cheek.

'Pa doesn't come out of there,' my eldest says quietly from the other side of me. 'He stays up above on a special platform.' The older boy looks at me to confirm and I nod. The little one nods, too, and tilts his head back to gaze at the big top of the tent. His rusty hair falls against my chin, and I bend to smell it. It doesn't calm me. He points again.

'That a swing.'

'It's a trapeze,' the girl says, and the little one shivers and turns his head towards her. I know his eyes are still pinned, though, to the metal swing high above the crowd. 'They go from that platform up there and work the trapeze,' the girl adds reluctantly, because the boy seems to be waiting.

'That where Pa sits,' he tells her. My eldest opens his mouth.

'No,' the girl answers first. My eldest sighs; the girl is slightly older than him. 'That's for the trapeze artists. Your dad is only a lighting man.' The boys shift uncomfortably around me.

'A lightning man?' the little one murmurs, but he doesn't

wait for an answer. He squeezes from my lap to draw with the lolly stick in the dirt. When I glance at the girl, she is blushing an unbecoming crimson. I want to pat her lacy knee.

The people fall quiet, but the ring remains the same. Children find their seats and whisper. The lolly man bawls a few more times and then tucks himself into a chair at the front. The thick dust that has been churned for hours clumps and settles so that the tent lights become clear and bright. My worry rises up my chest and sticks in my neck. I hiccough quietly, glad the little one is absorbed in his drawing. I glance again at the lolly man and wish that I could go to him for a drink, just one. The little one bounds off towards the tunnel. Two of the boys bring him struggling back, and I call him 'little fish' and smooth his legs on mine.

'The show is about to start,' the girl says to no one. Little stops wriggling and takes up staring at her hair.

When the tent lights begin to dim, we quickly face the front to see the empty ring with its colourful edging fade. The bright dirt turns to black. The people in the seats down below become murky and head-shaped. I feel the little one turn and rest against me. The boys perch in the darkness on the wooden bench on one side, the girl to the left, nearest the tunnel. I see what she means: we will be last to see the show as it comes out from that dark place, and then we will see only the backs and sides of the performers. Though Jo has told me that they perform in the round so that everyone gets a turn, I can see that they might angle the show to the highest payers, who will sit with their hands folded like the girl's and clap only at the end. I stop myself from looking up to where Jo said he would be, high above in the tent top behind a little flap. Knobs and buttons and switches for lights — he said he only has a tiny lamp to see so that the tent can be as dark as dark before the start of the show. He has dimmed the house lights. I imagine I can make out a lamp glow coming from the top of the tent, but of course, there's nothing. Just the little boy on my lap, breathing through his mouth, and my other sons muttering and nudging each other beside me.

We hear the drum best, being so close to the tunnel. It starts beneath us and gets louder and louder. Little one covers his ears and looks up at me so I wonder how his eyes can shine when there isn't any light. The drum roll fills the tent, and I think of Jo up there looking for the lights. Why must he be so high? What if the lamp goes? The drum continues until the lights go up, Jo told me. There are cues, it's an illusion. I think of the whiskey and both wish for it and doubt that we should have had it at all. There is no movement from the girl. What must she think? If Jo falls, they will smell it on his breath. The drum is so loud now it might be my heartbeat. The little one sits on my knee like a warm rock. And then a voice, like from God, fills the air.

'Ladies and gentlemen, boys and girls: the greatest show on earth. Watch the bearded lady ride the two-headed donkey. See the vicious lions roar and attack the very man who feeds them. Wonder at the acrobats on their flying trapeze.' Little, who has uncovered his ears, jolts on my lap at this. He looks up through the darkness towards the swing. 'Sit back in terror and delight and prepare for the wonder and the mystery of Maximillian's Magic Circus!'

Jo said that the drum would roll only until the lights go

up, but the blackness and the awful ratter-tat go on and fill my lungs like no smoke I have ever known. And he has failed, my Jo. Up there fumbling for the lights with the whole show waiting for him. They will be off without us in the painted van. One behind for the children. I feel the dirt on my feet and my thighs and the wooded chip of our rented floor and the little one growing to know only this. My thought is so quiet that even the boys don't pick it, so transfixed they are by the terrible rolling. In this heat and darkness no one hears. That I could cry so ridiculously surrounded by my dry-faced children! What must she think? Little one seems to have fallen asleep — his legs dangle and bump my knees as I shake.

The girl's voice cuts through the blackness, so close that her clean white teeth are almost in my ear. A soft curl, as though a bird has landed, gently knocks my streaming cheek. 'They do this to build suspense.' Through the dark I can just make out her head nodding at me. 'It's so that the ladies will be frightened and the men ... your ... Jo ...' She nods again. The drum, which has been going on the same way, I'm sure, since I was a girl, reaches some sort of crescendo and stops. The sticky, dirty tent is filled with a silence far worse than the drumming, and I wonder that the girl could be so wrong. A cold, unwilling finger touches the back of my hand. She is sorry, I think, and it's alright, she's just a girl. Come to us because we're the only ones left. 'Just wait,' she says to the nothingness.

Light. The sound comes like an electric thump. I have waited, and through my salted eyes there are a thousand bulbs shining all over the scoop of the tent. I am half-blind with it and turn, not towards my boys, but to the tunnel.

Struck as you might be by a penny or a pearl on the street. Before the little one jumps from my knee, and before the boys beside me hoot and wiggle like birds with snakes, and before the crowd and the ladies put their gloved and calloused hands together for the entire circus who pose in feathery, sparkled splendour in the once-empty ring, I see a flash of teeth, the fade of the girl's smile into the show light. Her hair brighter than all the bulbs in the circus.

AWAY WITH IT

They just fucking jumped the rise on this hill her whole body at the soft roof until the nicked little car landed fishtailing right past those sleeping houses and then on the other side of town slid into the lot and sprayed gravel over the tractors the cone glowing everyone laughing at the bouncing torchlight because it was such a crack that old man yelling like their dads about the cops the cops until he beamed into the backseat over her white skin.

'Jesus Christ.' He looked like he would cry.

NINE DAYS

Today it is winter. The houses close like clouds. And that sweet steam, how it drifts in from the unfilled swamp. Without our fence we get the thick of it — in the summer we were killing flies and now it's just the muck from the wetland in our noses. The flowers in the kitchen and in our room've gone bad; though Richard managed to put sugar in the water, their leaves curl, their petals brown at the edges. Last night the highway was an endless light beyond the darkness of the grass. We sat up in bed like old people or children. When the wind blows a certain direction, you can hear the trucks and cars slowing and starting again. Otherwise, it's just the television's flicker like pigment against all the windows. The sound of our staying still.

I had turned away from him on the bed, staring out at the pomegranate tree that tapped gently on the window of our room. The wind groaned outside, and the noise became insistent, the tree banging its scarlet fruit against the glass. In the morning, bloody, clotted prints, like paint on a fist, would mark the pane. The wind dropped and then rose again, suddenly, outside.

The body in the kitchen was almost featherless when I found it. Already pasted to the floor with blood. There are black and white and grey bits of down that swirl up in great loops when you move through them, all the way down to the bedroom and along the hall. They're all over me now — on my underpants and hair and clumped between my feet. The ducted heating slows and stops and then turns itself on again. We don't do anything, and it goes on and on. The space between one heartbeat and the lack of another.

The body heaved and its beak quivered; our eyes looked at each other as its heart shook like a rattle in my hand. An aeroplane shuddered the windows and the wineglasses. The cat's bell tinkled in its fur as she circled where I hunched on the ground with the bird. We all shook there. On the floor, beneath my hair, the chick rested in a knot of feet and flesh. Its smell was close, like an outside birth. Earth-stained and wind-flattened. The cat circled going *ca-ca-ca*. Jaws hung. And some howl came from me. The bloodied ball kicked a leg the colour of ripe fruit.

When it was dead, I thought how small it looked. How different to the other ones with wingspans and massive claws that scratched the lawn outside. It's vicious, the way they eat, and wipe their beaks on the power line, and eye off our heads as we walk. The cat may have risked her life to kill that bird for me. On the floor, the dust had begun to gather. It's a slow endless movement from roof to ground in these houses, and in the tight gap between the stove and wall, beads of grease dangle like web. Janine doesn't find them. She moves past on bare ankles and earrings and hands. Only a week ago she was flapping the mop over that bit of floor telling me that she'd had her Aden in the time it took to clean our house, and with less pain. I'd watched the water spread in pale circles over the floor and tried to imagine it. Now feathers stick to the bird blood and my blood and to the milk — a new white blood. They gave me an ice pack for the stitches that I forget to change. It swishes when I move.

When I first opened my eyes, it was afternoon, and for a moment the sun came through the window and onto the bed. I thought it must have been Cara crying that woke me. Small wild chirps that came from very near and then moved further and further away. At first, I didn't know what they could have meant. A mother might have. My eyes hurt, and I forgot what I had heard until it came again in the eerie light. A crying out. And I knew that it was her on the end of the bed, calling to me when I couldn't move. The cat came; I watched her circle, her great tail lashing her sides, and felt a moment of relief when the crying grew louder and then suddenly stopped. It started up again, but at intervals down the hall. I could barely hear it — I could pretend and go back to sleep. How guilt hurts!

When Richard and I were learning each clunk and scrape of the house, I thought I could never get used to it and hate it, as I had with our rentals. The door creaks; Richard worries but will never fix it. The way the benches look when they are wiped. The view through the tree over the grass and swamp from our window. If the frogs are breeding and the highway is quiet, all I can hear is the morning (and it's so misty, from the rain last night and the clouds today) and the wild earnestness of the wet land. I know it ends; I can see the highway lights from the window. But I also have a false memory of what it must have been like when there was only grass. And the hill or the tree or the clearing, rather than the lights of the cars or the power pole or the road. There are crows and magpies everywhere today, but even they, with their beaks cocked to the sky, seem ill at ease. Now I feel there is blood on the walls, not just on the bed and down the hallway floor. I heard the cat drag the bird away, calling its muffled *ca-ca-ca*. When I opened my eyes again, the green-tiled light of the clock read 2:17pm, and I knew that I had forgotten my baby.

It is Wednesday. Cold light coats the walls. I had forgotten her, now I remember. I am alone in the day now, where before I screamed in the kitchen (next door the children might have stopped playing, someone might have raised their blind). The little thing sat in my hands beneath my lank hair. A magpie — they come without wind. On wings, on wings — and children throw chunks of raw meat that they grab, that they watch with bright black eyes. Ages ago I used to hate them; I knew they came for the frogs that echo so vulnerably in the swamp there, and Richard and I would run out to wave the birds away. Running out across the field with the biting grass on our legs. And then someone told us there were snakes and so we stayed away and hoped they'd soon fill it in. The people with kids were frightened, and we were, too. But I have never seen a snake here, not even a skin. The dead little bird made me silent. They eat the snakes, too, I think. We were waving away a process, maybe an evolution. I stuck the bird up on the bench and held the cat until she struggled and bit. She nips my calf if I'm too slow with her food. She watched the bench then, to see if it moved. I watched, too, and wished it would. That beak would never hunt the frogs or snakes. It was too awful. That she would never grow.

Pulling myself from the floor was like pushing water; parts of me leak and journey down. When Mum was nursing her colleagues would come over for parties, at different times because of the shift work, and still smelling like the ward. They'd kiss our faces, Danny's and mine. I would first smell the makeup, and then the smell of the clean-sick, and then, sometimes, a death. They told me it was good, hard work they were doing. I could smell those hospital sheets on my skin, so I didn't stay in as long as they wanted. Richard wondered, he was distraught and tired, if the miscarriage did anything to cause it, and I said I didn't drink, it was the drink that did it back then. He looked sad. We looked at my womb and wondered.

•

I wished it were night and it was. I said, *I wish we sat in the park*, and we did so. Above the toilet block was a round concrete roof — quite beautiful with glass bricks, all clean and washed. The big trees hanging over them and the police station was just across from us — did we see them? I met them only twice, once to get my bicycle marked with their special gun. Once because I wagged school and smoked in that old, abandoned place. I said I was going to the doctor and looked so frightened that they let me go. They didn't bother, I noticed, with Diane. What we drank that night was vodka or gin — it was years before I heard the old wives' tale about gin in a hot bath. Well, it must have been hot, but I didn't notice the weather. Spoon came, and we all got drunk. Diane and I got involved in a discussion about who wanted to pash him. Spoon seemed not able to believe his ears (which stuck out; he had that red English face and an accent that we thought sexy, baggy jeans, a cigarette in his hand). He probably wanted us to be fair and both do it — but I won. For one night I won. And Spoon seemed only a little disappointed. Before the party and after the gin, I whispered at Diane in the toilet. It seemed we were the only ones in the world, though Spoon was probably still on the roof with the other guy. I vomited with her hand holding my hair and said, 'I haven't had my period.' Diane looked wise. Everything seemed clean as I washed my face. Is it possible? Only sixteen years old and public toilets were clean? No graffiti? No piss on the wall? No one's tampon on the floor? Diane might have asked me how long it had been or I might have told her, but she definitely said, 'You must be preggas', and we would have laughed nervously and knowledgeably. Both wanting and dreading it. Two years later Diane would be, and then, a year after, again. With Heath from my maths class, a nice guy and a bogan. Diane and I wrote each other songs, almost love songs, during that time.

At the party I pashed Spoon against the glass wall of the house. The people on the inside would have seen his back. The people on the outside would have seen mine. His girlfriend watched us and there was a commotion, a crying. Silly, naughty girl. I'm lucky I didn't get slapped. Then, nothing. I went home with Diane (of course — the master of disguise). In the morning, she would go and tell my father about the books we'd read; Spoon went home with his girlfriend. I woke in the doona on Diane's floor. Years later, Diane would ask me if I was a dyke after I told her I'd shaved my head and didn't have a boyfriend. 'Last time you rang,' she said, 'you didn't have a boyfriend.' It was proof to her.

When I woke on Diane's floor I didn't have a boyfriend either. He had dumped me for the nth time, perhaps that week (time, it moved then). Much later, Marc would tell me that as he was the last Freeman, he basically needed an heir. But at that time, he had dumped me, and I woke on the floor with blood on my legs. Diane's aunt's bathroom smelled like Toilet Duck, Blue Loo, and potpourri air freshener. A yellow frilled toilet mat coated the floor. The light through the window was Victoria in the early spring, morning, impossibly bright. Cool, still, in the toilet room. Although there was a lot of blood, I picked out the pale broad bean nestled among the red on the crotch of my undies. Straight away. There is a calm that comes with teenage hangovers. A maturity. And then you regress. I stared at it a while and thought about the amount of blood. And then there was the gin. The period that came so late. I went back to Diane and told her, and she looked at me with horror. Diane was not a girl from a good family — her parents had dumped her with her aunt and called her a slut. She had been hit and yelled at. She thought she could recall something sexual. A cousin? 'I guess it couldn't handle the rough night,' I said and laughed. And Diane eyed me while she faltered for comforting words. I suppose I went home. I suppose I called Marc — though it could have been hours, days later. I know I told him. I know he said, 'At least you're not pregnant.' I know I reminded him of that later when he was trying to get back together. I know I was strange the days after, not from the emotion (to be pregnant then! now! the reality of it was horror), but I was shaken. Like something, a cladding, had been pulled away.

When Stacey came to me and told me that she and Stephen had fought on the weekend, I said, 'I think I had a miscarriage', and she halted and stared. I cried a little because I was supposed to and weaved up the road to the school, dizzy, out of breath. I was vaguely aware of people knowing. Of that eyeing off and watching. And then, weeks later, my confirmation.

We were moved to a different room for the lesson in a heat wave that I noticed. We sat on tables at the back with our sticky legs adhering to the tops. Some of us had spray bottles of water and doused ourselves throughout the class. One of the fans didn't work. The lesson was on the fetus. We were supposed to watch the documentary and fill out the sheet. But I was having trouble. The screen took up the entire room — and everywhere at once was the small bean I'd seen just weeks before in Diane's aunt's loo. A six- to eight-week-old fetus. Inedible. Nondescript. Feeling nothing and everything was scientific proof. Where *I think* becomes *I have. I haven't* becomes *I had.* And gin or chance steps in to give you another turn around. And then I am thirty. Blood in a house in the cold with my wrists exposed like beams. Where Richard is, they hold Cara as I held the bird.

'Were you still asleep?'

'No. I got up. Made coffee.'

'Good. I'll be home soon. Have you eaten?'

'Just the coffee.'

'Then I'll get you something. Soup?'

'Mmm.'

'You alright?'

'Yes, I'm alright. Are you with her now?'

'The autopsy. I've arranged the funeral for Friday. Nine days.'

'Nine days.'

•

The room is like a temple with bells ringing and the white cloud light refracting off every wall. You could be either trapped or secluded in here, on the far side from the highway, with a glimpse across the fence to the little road where people let their dogs pee on the lawn. The ducted heating hummed on and moved warm air up through the vent beside my feet as I opened the door. A few of the feathers drifted in. Others were stuck with blood and flapped gently. I closed the door and found I could lock it. *Anything I sit on will be bloody now.* Wraps; a pram; a cot with sides you can lower so it's just like a bed; clothes for every possibility of what might be her — the handed-down dresses, the miniature overalls, the jumpsuits. Everything so white, like we knew she wouldn't make it. We had no name for a girl, though Richard was set on Samuel. Cara for diamond, darling, dear. A stillness in the suburb, as though you block something off and keep it protected. I couldn't live anymore by the window with the trams screaming past my feet, the big, towering electric lines — you're not supposed to touch the one just outside.

And I always enjoyed the little birds that came to sit here. One morning a pigeon tapped on the roof and looked at me with a startled, embarrassed expression. *What am I doing here? How did I come?* When I sneezed, it flailed around with its wings everywhere and flopped off towards some other rooftop. Now, with the fence before me. It should be the perfect suburban setting for my baby — out the window through the flyscreen, the cheap pine board, the other brick house of the same design only metres away (the toilet here and the toilet there have views of each other — it's best to shut the blinds), the blue, grey, purple, and white sky. It is so much like a home.

Richard bought whiskey, and we've kept it here until she was born so we could drink it together. Nine months, he said, was long enough to age a whiskey. I told him we'd be plastered from the first sip — it had been so long — but he was so happy and so longed for it to be opened. He used to tell my stomach to hurry up. He was ready to open that bottle. The first sniff is like acid to your nose. The people who drink lots of the stuff must have no nasal hair — it fills the space like a fly, moving into every stream of light and throwing itself at the window. The roar of it. If a neighbour passed, I would hide it quickly under the cot — to drink the birth whiskey in your child's room! And with Cara only kilometres away. Only days dead. And without my husband, as though I could celebrate alone. When I spoke to someone from the centre, they said that losing her was losing family, that the memories might not be present, but the hopes were. She told me to articulate, to name. Darling, diamond, dear. And Richard so sure she would be Samuel.

This is the house before the swamp. The light has gone from Cara's side — from our room, we can see the edges of blue and amber and pink glint from the tops of cars (if you're driving, you have to flap down your sunshield against it) but here in Cara's place it is already darkened. Our fence and our neighbour's fence just a dirty blue against the wall. The cat scratches at the door. The door chimes and then thumps. The woman from up the road, bearing armfuls of food for which Richard will be grateful. How can I eat? If I don't hide the whiskey, I will hide myself — everything and the feathers from the bird. Melissa? Mel? And then she would bring more food. Her husband would clap Richard around the neck and sigh. They would say I'm not coping. I am under the cot. I have the birth whiskey and I can drink now. Richard will come and try to make coffee again. He will want to know why I am in here without him with the whiskey and the blood. He will want to know why I can't open the cupboard doors and see all those little hangers. I might scream if he tries to. He hates dead things and will be angry about the bird. No. No, he won't. He is Richard. He buys whiskey for pregnant women. He is grateful for casserole and organises funerals for his child. He's not festering and leaking here on the carpet.

Wear white. If I were a baby, I would wear white to my funeral — people will say that I'm happy if I dress her in things too bright. But white? I should know this answer. I've only to open the cupboard to see. Mum sent us woollens, deep greens and browns and reds — the colour of the grass and the earth and the blood. And we have the billowy onesies and summer dresses, all too big and still and cotton. The trees are skeletal. The grass in the morning is stiff and pale. In the laundry, our breath is vapour. Cara must be warm on the day, but the jumpsuits are second hand. Someone else's names are written on the tags. On one of the toes is a tiny tear, but I had bought it anyway, believing it would be good enough for a baby (they grow so fast! she will be in and out of it before we can blink!). Outside the fence begins to glow with the streetlight. The banging starts and again stops. Melissa thinks I'm in here. She thinks I'm asleep — it's what she would do. She won't leave the casserole to be got by the cat, and I should go and thank her. I should tell her to keep close her children.

And so here is the silence. When the night comes and there are no footfalls in the hall. The cat has crept outside for some prey — she will never eat cat food again. All this blood. My teeth chatter, though the heating pumps on. With the door closed, it seems pressurised. If Cara were here, I might worry, but I am. Here. And Richard has not returned. The whole room is an orange silky light that makes my arm freckles look huge and contagious. When I shift, the dried blood yanks my hair and stitches. When the phone rings, I cannot move. Where are the telephones in every room? The hot showers and someone to hold your arms? Cara, I have crept here.

I didn't feel with the miscarriage. I was relieved, joyous even. I dyed my hair blonder and felt that something serious had happened to me. Something important. I was young, but that wasn't it. I was not in a white house with a cat and a marriage and payments to make. I was not thirty and sobbing for someone to come. But I was drinking. I was laughing, holding a tune.

Ahh now, here is my husband in the driveway. Here now are the yellow lights on the fence. Here is the ding of the car door opening and then the bang of it closed. The tweet of the lock, his hurried footfalls on the path. Here are his keys in the door, oh, he dropped them, try again! But I'm not ready. I'm too big under our cot, bulbous. Drenched. The cupboard — Richard calls my name through the dark of the house. We've not yet played this game. The whiskey sloshes against the bottle and catches the orange light in its amber.

How guilt hurts! The crash of the cot and the change table and the shelf. The groan of the curtains I clutch together. Richard's voice is hollow, dry. As though he has seen her die again today. I only felt her; he saw the blueness of her crown that never changed to a living pinkish skin. White. Yes, white is perfect, we must have a white dress somewhere. Richard might know, but no. I must find a white dress for my child.

A song that I have hardly heard spreads through my mind in here. A song about darkness. It is a highway song. A song to be sung alone with the lights of the car switched off and only the wind beating around you. Gradually things get light and then lighter. Your eyes adjust, and it feels as though you might be going, just slowly, though you can feel the car body move, your foot presses down and down. It is like that in here — the light from the street helps, but I can also see the dresses deep in the dark of the cupboard. And hear the hangers clang. Richard can hear them, too; he is silent and then calls out. Wait a minute, I say — not sure if he heard. And then I see it: the darkness. All that swaying around and here is a yellow dress that a friend has lent us, that I love. Would she want it back if I wanted to bury my baby in it? Her next child would never be the same if they wore it knowing. Does my staring at it make it unwantable? I am sure. Just our having it would make it different. A yellow dress that I love that I have chosen myself. There is birth whiskey left for Richard should he want it. He has slumped against the door. I can hear the weight of his back against it. He can cry. I can bleed on the floor. Cara's hair and fingernails can continue to grow in the hospital only kilometres away. In nine days, she will be gone.

REAL

Craig Henderson. You are the most attractive real estate agent in the region. When 47-year-old Jessica and I see your sign on the highway, on the bus station, above the takeaway, we think about retirement. We tuck our chippies in our jackets and remember the time we saw you at the fancy New World. Jessica told you your own name and I said how we never see you at PAK'nSAVE. You inclined your head, just like on the poster. We looked to see if savings fell out. You're set back from the road, Craig Henderson. You're close to schools, shops, and amenities. 'You've got a good heat pump, Craig Henderson,' Jessica whispers into the drizzled air at the bus stop billboard. The sign reads GET AHEAD and Jessica scratches JOB into the Perspex over your face with the key to our share house. If we don't, someone who doesn't understand you will. And, Craig Henderson? We have questions. Are you perfect for a family? Are you a first-time dream or an opportunity to upsize? Will we have no regrets? We've pooled our money. After the chips, we have fifteen dollars thirty cents in the hand and nine hundred and forty-one in the bank. But how much do you want, Craig Henderson? Your golden hands. Your reflective face. Our jackets stink of hot oil, but they're warm.

SMOKO

Four cigarette breaks. Joni took two of them, depending on her shift. She worked three of the early Deli shifts on Mondays to Thursdays and two late shifts, Friday to Sunday. The smoking break was in addition to a morning or afternoon tea and a lunch or dinner. The smokers ate quickly at the Deli staffroom table and then hurried out the back door, where there was an awning at the supermarket end of the staff car park.

Black pants or skirt below the knee and a red polo shirt with a white embroidered logo of a shopping trolley on its pocket. That was the uniform. The Checkout staff polos always looked brand new. They weren't allowed to knot them at the front to show their midriffs anymore but could wear their hair in a fountain or have as much fringe as they liked. In Deli, they parted their hair into severe buns to keep it out of the cold cuts. Joni's from-the-packet polo faded almost immediately in the billows of greasy steam from the rotisserie, and the hot wash at home with Ultracare heavy-duty laundry liquid to get rid of the smell. She pulled a clean shirt on in the staff toilets before each shift and she could still smell it: the pinky-grey devon luncheon rolls straight from the big refrigerator, the chickens spinning. That smell helped her get in the zone. Being in the zone was a reality and a mentality, Team Leader Charlotte told them in the cramped break room before they started for the day. If everyone was in the right zone, the Deli would run like a ship, all in their correct roles, turning to the customers with their best faces. Being in the zone was knowing exactly how many of the cheap sausages made up a kilo (sixteen) and adding an extra one in front of the customer after it was priced. Joni got a bag of those sausages at the end of her early shift with a staff discount — she was self-conscious about it — but then Charlotte said: 'A rich person will shop around no matter what you do, but give a poor person a free sausage? Forever.' Sarah, who did the cabinet arranging, thought that was very funny. For Joni, those sausages were a secret message to Charlotte: *I am a keeper*. She took them home so her mum, Carol, could do them all the different ways — fried, curried, stewed, pigs in blankets, cold from the fridge the next day.

The break room board roster sat beneath last year's calendar. Someone had crossed out 1994 and written '199T5' with the sign-in pen. The roster said that the cigarette break was for smokers only. It was impossible to fake it. Most of the managers smoked. Joni smoked a lot more now that she worked at the supermarket. Yas, who was in Deli for only a few months before she transferred to Bakery, had tried to argue that she was addicted to coffee and needed the extra break, too. Her application was turned down twice. It was a special group that took off their aprons and filed out when someone called 'smoko'. If it was busy, other team leader Liv would stay back to serve while the rest went out the back for their five-minute break. 'Should we wait?' one of the smokers would ask. Liv waved them on. *Have your smoko.*

Under the awning were three battered white plastic chairs with cigarette burns and gouge marks, beside a metal tray of sand and butts. Those who missed out on chairs or didn't want one stood or sat with their backs to the wall of the supermarket. Robin, who did the slicing, was of the opinion that if she sat down, she'd never want to get up again. They were always quitting the smokes and taking them up again. The awning shaded that spot all day — the beating sun never made it there — and sometimes a wind howled, hot or cooling. If you stood with your back against the wall, you could spend smoko watching the summer rain beat down. If a lighter had run out, they shared; they joked about brands. At first smoko, Joni always needed the bathroom, so by the time she pushed on the door to the car park Kate or Robin would be shouting, 'Hurry up, Winnie Blue! Three minutes and counting!' They'd cheer when she lit up and sucked back. She didn't feel anything when she was behind the Deli counter looking out at the mums pushing their endless babies in prams through the supermarket. But this smoking in a circle of others. *This* was being a woman.

Second smoko was different. They were tired. They'd had their day. They talked about the customers — a man who said three kilograms of champagne ham but meant 300 grams, and now they had to do a special on ham. If it was the early shift, they talked about their plans for after. Picking up the kids and taking them to Gran's. Grabbing a few things on the way out. Joni liked to get a Violet Crumble milkshake from the takeaway shop in the mall and catch the late bus home, telling Carol she'd stayed to clean up at work. There was another takeaway chicken place on the highway that did good blue heavens in a proper metal cup, but Joni had avoided it since she saw Sarah starting a shift there straight after her supermarket one. She didn't know how to acknowledge being so worn.

The all-staff meeting was on the Thursday Joni wasn't rostered. Thursday and Friday: a rare two days off in a row without losing the good double-time pay of Sunday — a sign, maybe, that Charlotte had noticed her staying power. Joni used those days to sort out the things of her dad's that Carol said were a bunch of old crap, although Carol still sat on the spare bed clutching an old brown cardigan, a shoebox, a newspaper clipping about Dad winning big at the dogs. Carol called him up and held a fierce whispered conversation — the phone cord stretched to its limit across the hall.

'Did he want to talk to me?' Joni asked.

'No, he did not.' Carol told her to throw it all away. Joni packed most of it back in the boxes and stacked them in the laundry cupboard. She would have been compensated an hour's pay if she went in for the Thursday all-staff but Carol told her it wasn't worth the forty-five-minute walk there and back or the bus fare.

'Time is money,' Carol said and pointed with a long purple nail at the TV where a game show was playing. A woman in a snakeskin dress revealed a new settee.

Joni went for a walk along the storm drain reserve. She didn't take her smokes — sometimes the house was so filled with it. A black swan glided along the murky surface. Joni wondered if it was lost. It looked so serene. When she started her Saturday shift, she looked forward to telling everyone about the swan. Even if they thought it was funny. As it was, there was no chance for it. Smoko was announced and Joni filed out with the smokers. She was wondering whether to begin with the swan or build up to it when she passed a new sign next to the break sheet printed on yellow paper. Blocked Sarah's way staring at it.

'What's that?' Joni asked.

'Oh my fucking god, Joni. She doesn't know!' Sarah pushed past, pulling Joni along with her. 'Joni doesn't know!' she announced through the door that led to the huddle of Kate, Liv, and Robin outside.

Liv pointed her cigarette at Joni. 'That's right, you were off. How was it?'

But Robin was talking, waving her cigarette around in puffy trails. 'They're taking away smoking. Right at the end of the meeting, in *other business*. '"Oh yeah, and by the way, we're taking away smoking"'.

'Fucking Charlotte,' said Kate.

'How is it Charlotte?' With only two minutes to go, Liv lit another cigarette off the first and sucked.

'*You* know.'

'Anyway.' Liv breathed a dragon. 'They're not banning smoking. Just smoko.'

'What about smoko?' Joni asked. She'd forgotten to light up and scrambled for her blue packet. It wasn't in her pants pocket. She looked around. The ground was scattered with butts that had missed the tray. Liv handed over one of her Longbeaches and a lighter.

'They're saying smoko "offers an unfair advantage".' Liv

held up her smoking hand at the protests. 'No, Robin, it's true. Healthier workplace etcetera etcetera. I mean, it's real.'

'Those corporate cunts got me addicted in the first place!' Kate yelled.

'Alright, Special K.' Liv ground her cigarette into the sand, which was a sign for them all to do so.

'We've got to fight this,' said Kate.

'Sure thing. In your afternoon break.'

Joni was on rotisserie in the afternoons and did the whole two rows of chooks — seven for each metal rod — without stuffing. It was too late once the machine was blasting and rolling them around. She watched them twist and scald, knowing they were empty not just of their original insides but of the seasoned filling that made them better. Sarah knocked her with an elbow.

'Hello? Serving?'

The woman on the other side of the counter wanted to pre-order two chickens because the family was suddenly coming to their house after the race, and while she was up for making a potato salad, she was not doing a whole roast.

'With or without stuffing?' Joni asked her. 'Without is popular ...' The woman gave her a look. Joni couldn't bite her nails through the gloves. She clicked the clicker meant for counting chickens until Sarah told her to stop. It was very rare for someone to take a toilet break outside of break time that went a little too long, coming back flushed from the outside, smelling of smoke. They would never do it under Charlotte, and even Liv didn't like it. It was an unspoken rule, like taking two lunches. Joni removed her rubber gloves and the fat-slick rubber apron she wore for rotisserie. In the bathroom she sat on the loo looking up at the ventilation window with an unlit smoke in her mouth. By the time afternoon tea came around, Joni had her cigarette out before she was halfway out the door. Sarah had the same afternoon tea break, and she was already there, listening to her discman on one of the plastic chairs and eating a vanilla slice she wasn't likely to share. Joni didn't usually bring morning or afternoon tea. At first she had accepted whatever was offered by the others, but one day a look between Kate and Robin stopped her as she reached out for a pink chunk of finger bun. They still offered, but Joni said no unless it was a birthday and they were in a break room, with paper plates and an iced cake in a white box from the bakery. Sarah moved her headphones to her neck and pushed a chair towards Joni with her foot.

'What's Kate going to do about smoko?' asked Joni, sitting down beside her.

Sarah said, 'Kate?' around a flaky mouthful of slice. She swallowed. 'Why would Kate do anything?'

'She was so mad. She said we have to do something.'

Sarah laughed. 'Kate won't do shit. No one will.' A few weeks back they were all talking about how it was bad to eat and smoke at the same time, because your tastebuds were open and the smoke got in and gave you tongue cancer. Sarah wrapped up the final bit of slice in a paper bag stamped with the chicken shop logo before lighting up. Everyone knew that Sarah wanted to work in Bakery. She'd been seen in a nice shirt and a small plaster over her nose ring going into the Bakery staff area on her day off, and then showing up for her usual shift at the Deli the next day and every day she was rostered after. The women who worked in Bakery were strong-looking, like Sarah, but they had freshly scrubbed faces. Sarah looked like she'd just come straight from a night club to work. She didn't smell or anything. She just had that look.

'It's the eye makeup,' Joni heard Kate saying once.

At the dinner break Joni took off her apron and went over to Bakery to buy a single white roll on her staff credit. Then she returned to the Deli and took the bits of chicken that had fallen off, or been mangled after a customer's cut, and put them on the roll. She ducked her head so that customers wouldn't think she was available. One called out, but Kate stepped in with a booming, 'How can I help you?' Joni shot her a grateful look and Kate nodded firmly. It was what they did at the Deli. If time wasn't money, it was at least important. Joni took the open sandwich through to the staff area and the big cool room that came off it. The shared condiments were kept in a tray by the door. Charlotte and Liv had a big blow up about the condiments not long after Joni started. Charlotte said it was unhygienic and took the matter upstairs, but management investigated and found that the Bakery, Deli, and Loading Bay staffrooms all had a condiments tray of sorts, and most of the division managers argued it was good for morale. There were other things: Bakery staff got free buns for their meal breaks, Deli staff got free leftover meats that couldn't be sold, and the Fruit and Veg people got anything with spots. This raised the issue of the Checkout staff — what did they get? Management had to allow Checkout staff to get a little of each free thing then

— a bun, a bit of chicken, some lettuce and tomatoes if there were some, a banana — enough to make up a sandwich. Then everyone said how unfair it was that the Checkout staff got a whole sandwich when the rest of the staff only got pieces and had to buy the rest, so management conceded that the staff in sections could keep their special tray in the cool room with condiments provided from the supermarket shelves, within reason. If Checkout staff wanted condiments, they had to buy their own. People said Charlotte was in the bad books after that — the whole thing had caused management more than a headache.

'Serves her right, stuck up mole,' Kate had muttered.

But Liv said Charlotte would just find another way to impress them upstairs. 'She knows what she wants, I'll give her that.'

Joni chose the mayonnaise from the tray and took it to the staff table to spread on her bread. They were out of lettuce at home, and she didn't want to take up her dinner break finding one in Fruit and Veg. Unlike the Bakery and Deli, where you could purchase with staff credit at the counters, anything from Fruit and Veg had to go through the checkout. Checkout staff dropped their charm and rang it through with barely a word when they saw the red of a supermarket T-shirt. Joni thought their mouths must get so sore from smiling. If you were tired in the Deli you could turn to the slicer and buy yourself some time arranging the devon or twiggy sticks while others served. Checkout staff were on the front line with their giant ponytails. Still. Joni wiped a drip that had landed on the side of the mayonnaise bottle and put the jar back in the cool room. They were meticulous about their tray. It was their win. Outside it was dark but warmer than in the supermarket. Joni stretched out on one of the chairs and ate the sandwich. No one else was doing dinner. They must have gone up to the takeaways. A forklift with its lights on zoomed past at the end of the staff car park.

Joni caught the bus home after night shifts even when the air was syrupy warm for a walk because Carol told her there were rapists out there. The Friday night connection was only seven minutes after work ended and Joni often missed it — forty minutes until the next. On Saturday nights the bus left at 9:20, so Joni didn't have to rush cleaning the rotisserie with the oven cleaner spray and scourer — so mangled by the end with grease and chemicals it had to be thrown away. She wandered up to the bus stop on the highway and had time for a cigarette before it arrived.

Carol was watching TV, in her armchair that backed onto the kitchen. It was a Saturday night movie about a police dog and officer duo, but it didn't really matter what it was about. Carol watched everything. Other people watched everything, too, but they didn't take it in. They just stared at the TV or had it on in the background for company. Carol *really* watched. She didn't have a favourite channel, she didn't flick. She studied the TV guide, settled on something, and watched it through. Her programme was always about to start. Joni's dad had bought Carol a video player that she used to tape *Neighbours* when Joni was on shift, but she preferred her TV in the moment. One morning it would be the election coverage in a different country. By mid-morning a talk show. Then a soap. A cartoon. A documentary about

whale seals. The news. A movie. Hours of tele-sales. A
church service. That was how Carol knew about rapists and
all the other things she warned Joni about. The dog on the
TV was going to die — they had seen it before. Joni went
to wash her hair. She smelled it when she got out for any
traces of chicken, then put her uniform in the wash basket
in the laundry. The laundry was a liminal space. Robin, who
went to art college, talked about liminal spaces: where things
couldn't be categorised. The laundry held the washing and
some pot plants. A cupboard with cleaning things, and food
for a cat that had since disappeared, paper and coloured
pencils from when Joni was small, a collection of jars, some
cooking pots with too wobbly handles, Joni's dad's boxes,
video tapes, old cassettes and a whole bunch of Carol's nail
polish that wasn't in daily use. Anything that didn't fit into
other places went in the laundry room. Joni pushed these
things aside to get to a jumbo drawing pad and a pencil case
stuffed so full it couldn't close.

At the kitchen table, she sat with her back to Carol and
the TV and chose a red pencil.

'What's that?' Carol asked when the movie had ended
and ads were playing. Joni sat back and looked at the paper.
A red mass — patchy in places — with lettering.

'It's a sign.'

Carol fetched her cigarettes from the TV table. 'A sign
for what?'

'They're banning smoko.'

'They're banning what?' Carol shot over to the table in a
blast of smoke.

'Smoko. The smoking break.'

'They are not.'

When Carol turned her attention to something her eyes blazed. Usually that focus was trained on the TV. Joni shrank from the attention but she also felt its warmth. She picked up the pencil again.

'The corporates upstairs say it's unhealthy. And unfair. On non-smokers, you know.'

Carol stabbed at the paper with her ring finger. 'And what's that?'

'It's a protest.' Joni's cigarettes were all the way in her bedroom. Carol and Joni didn't smoke each other's brand, no matter what. 'I'm going to protest. "Save our smoko".'

Carol sat back and took her in. 'Stand around outside the supermarket with this on a stick?'

'I'll put it up in the break room. Next to the break sheet.'

Carol took a drag and blew it out. 'You're going about it the wrong way.' Joni wanted to cover the sign. It was too much now, that intensity. It would burn her up along with the paper. 'What you need,' Carol continued, 'is a petition. I saw them do it on TV. All these workers in America. It wasn't a supermarket. It was a factory making chocolate products, Easter eggs and everything. The owners wanted to roster shorter shifts so they wouldn't have to pay for breaks. Two-and-a-half-hour shift, then another, then another. Back-to-back. Anyway, the workers made a petition.'

'Did they win?'

'They won.'

Carol smoothed the sign with her palm, purple nails and smoke held aloft. 'That will draw attention to your cause. Then you write' — she dug around in the pencil case until she found a permanent marker — '"Sign the petition!" here, like this. And you stick the petition below, see?'

'And the petition has everyone's names?'

Carol shook her head. 'You can't do that. You need for people to come to it of their own free will. To show they really believe in it. Get me a ruler, love.' The ruler wasn't in the laundry. Joni found it in the sideboard in the hall, where the bills were stacked. By the time she got back, Carol had written 'Petition' in large black letters over the top of a new piece of jumbo paper that she'd cut in half with kitchen scissors. She used the ruler to make neat lines all over the page with a black pencil, and then made sections for 'name' and 'signature'. There was a space at the top between the heading and the lines. The late talk show started on the TV, but Carol was absorbed in the paper. 'This is where you put the details of the petition so that people know what they're signing. You draft it first to get it right.'

Carol pushed the other half of the cut paper across the table. Joni found a grey-lead pencil in the case and wrote, *This is a petition for people to protest about the banning of smoko. We want to fight for smoko because it is an important break for smokers. It isn't fair to change it suddenly.*

'Fetch my glasses, love.' Carol bent over the paper and wrote notes. Then she composed a new sentence beneath. *Join us to fight the unfair changes to our smoking break! Banning smoko is discriminatory! Save our smoko!* 'See, it's what you said, but more personal. And you repeat your slogan — that's a good slogan, Joni — to reinforce it in people's heads.' Carol copied the paragraph to the petition in neat handwriting. They positioned it under the sign.

'Now I put it up in the Deli staffroom?'

Carol's eyes glinted. '*Now* we make copies to post in every staff room in the supermarket. We *could* get it photocopied at the library. But they'd be black and white.'

Carol ripped off another jumbo sheet for Joni, passed her
the red pencil, and started on a new petition.

Managers had permanent positions on the payroll. Charlotte
tended not to work weekends; it was always Liv. You could
say to Liv, 'I'll be back in a tick', and she would nod and
trust you. Joni skipped her dinner break and scrubbed the
rotisserie with a ferocity and speed that had it shining.
She waited right through until it was nearly the end of
her shift, then got her bag from the break room hook and
took it over to the all-staff room where the Fruit and Veg,
Checkout staff, and managers took their breaks, and where
the Nightfill and Delivery staff put their belongings. The
supermarket was closed, and the Checkout staff had all gone
home. It was just the other divisions cleaning. The Nightfill
staff would arrive soon to stack the shelves. Joni found a
space on the notice board between the break sheet and an
old flier for the Christmas party. She pinned up the poster
and stuck the petition beneath it. The supermarket red was
bright and powerful. Anyone looking at the board would
see it. She crossed the supermarket to the Bakery and let
herself into the tiny staffroom there. Bakery started their
shifts early in the morning, to get the doughs baked. After
4pm they packaged and priced the remaining bread, and
put it out in baskets for people to take for themselves up to
the cash registers. Joni had to move a few notices to fit the
poster and petition on the small board. Back in the Deli, Liv
was still cleaning up. Robin was sick and had gone home, so
Joni helped Liv by washing the slicer parts, drying them, and

putting the machine back together. At 9pm, Liv was sitting
at the break room table doing the rosters. Joni washed a cup
that had been left in the sink. Liv was still there. Joni got
out the poster from her bag and, with Liv watching, posted
it on the break room board. She moved a notice about free
kittens to the top — they were all rehomed anyway, it was all
everyone had talked about three weeks ago. Carol and Joni
hadn't taken one in the end. Their last cat had peed behind
the TV and shorted the electrics. There was still a smell.

'You going to sign that?' Liv asked, sitting back from the
roster.

'I thought I'd let others go first —'

'As the author. "Petition by Joni" sort of thing.'

Joni stared at the space at the bottom of the petition.

'You'd better own it,' Liv said. 'Management will be more
pissed if they have to spend time working out who.' Liv
turned back to the roster. Joni got a pen from the sign-in
book and wrote 'Petition by Joni Laing' at the bottom. She
hurried through the other staffrooms to do the same, then
ran for her bus.

Sarah gave Joni sparkle eyes from the olive buckets when
Joni arrived for her shift on Monday morning. Joni couldn't
tell if it was a happy sparkle or a dangerous one. The break
room was still empty. Joni put on her apron and saw, as she
passed, that Liv had added her name to the petition. On the
way through the plastic swing doors, she nearly ran flat into
Charlotte, who stared like she didn't know Joni at all.

'Who did the pack-down last night?' Charlotte finally
asked. 'You, Liv and ... Robin? There's no need to stack the

olive buckets way up so high if we just have to get them down again in the morning. I flagged that at the last meeting. Are the sausages out? I want that display kale nice and straight today.' She clapped her hands like she was in a workout video and shouted to maybe no one or maybe to Joni and Sarah, 'Today is going to be a big day. A good day! Let's go!' At some point, Sarah added her name to the petition, and so did Kate and the new woman, Holly, whose high-school-aged daughter had also started working the weekends. When Joni went to Bakery to get a roll at lunch time, two of the women there told her they'd signed and both managers had, too, even though one didn't even smoke. She went into the supermarket proper and gathered two packets of spiral pasta, an on-special carbonara sauce and some fruit and vegetables, including an iceberg lettuce the size of a volleyball, and took them to the checkout. The woman there had an *Alison* name tag. She flicked her eyes from Joni's faded red shirt to her face and paused mid-punch of the register keys.

'Are you Joni? The one with the sign? Oh, I've stuffed up.' She lifted a phone for assistance. While they waited Joni told her that she was the one. 'All the guys in Fruit and Veg are signing it. They love a union. Hey Steve,' Alison said to the team leader who'd come over, 'this is Joni. The one with the sign.'

'Troublemaker!' Steve grinned. He leaned his shoulder into Alison's. 'Keys, *then* shoot the breeze.'

'Whatever, Steve. And anyway, she's famous!'

Steve grinned and Alison chatted to Joni while she bagged the lettuce.

'Good luck!' Alison called as Joni went back towards the Deli. Carol had reminded her it was good to set a time limit to the petition. So people understood the urgency, and so it could be presented to management in a timely fashion. At the end of her shift, Joni took a pen and went around to the petitions, adding a deadline for the end of the week. The Deli staffroom was free of Charlotte, and the only staff member in the Bakery waved her through. At the main staffroom, the shift change-over and break times had coincided. Fruit and Veg guys were sitting at the big break table with the Checkout staff; others were rummaging around the lockers. Joni took a breath and crossed the room with her pen to print the date on the sheet. The break room behind her grew quiet.

'What's she added?'

'A date. I don't see your name on there, Sok — you better hurry.'

'Good on you, Jody.'

Joni smiled at them and nodded.

Sarah said she'd go with Joni upstairs to the management offices to submit the petition on their Friday dinner break. At 6:30 they took off their aprons and their tight hairbands and went around to the divisions to remove the petitions and signs. There weren't many more names on the Deli and Bakery sheets — most of those staff had added their signatures early.

'You didn't think Charlotte would sign, did you?' Sarah laughed. She put her arm over Joni's shoulder and steered her through the supermarket towards the main staffroom. Joni had seen some of the older women arm-in-arm — especially at the end of the Bakery shift when they went off together, floury as dough. There were drinks that happened with Checkout staff, Fruit and Veg, and a couple of the managers. Charlotte went to step aerobics with two of the women from upstairs. Joni peered beyond Sarah's hand to see if anyone else noticed. One of the Fruit and Veg guys made a gesture by the bananas that Joni didn't catch but caused Sarah to flick her middle finger. The staffroom petition had so many signatures they'd run off Carol's neat lines. A new page — the back of another notice by management about the condition of the bathrooms — had been stuck up beside it to house the extras. Joni hadn't been up the stairs since she had her interview, and then once more to sign some forms for HR and collect her polo shirt. The stairwell was hot — an unairconditioned space with doors off it. Sarah sprang up the stairs in a way that reminded Joni of Carol. Three floors up, she paused.

'You ready?' Sarah straightened her shoulders and pushed back her hair. 'All business.'

'All business,' Joni agreed. Sarah opened the door and strode ahead down the carpeted corridor. They'd made an appointment with Aaron, the assistant regional manager, for 6:40pm. Aaron's door was closed but they could hear him speaking beyond it. Sarah couldn't stop laughing. She pressed her ear against the door and sniggered into her hand.

'Okay, maybe we just go?' Sarah turned to leave. Joni looked at the red signs and carefully arranged petitions. She knocked. The speaking stopped. The door was flung open. Joni knew who Aaron was now she saw his face. He never spoke at meetings but nodded a lot. He wasn't one of the managers who had drinks. Joni had seen him in soccer gear. Aaron took in their faded polos.

'Yes?'

'We have an appointment with Aaron Jenson at 6:40pm,' Joni told him.

'One moment,' Aaron said. He stepped back into the office and picked up a small tape recorder. 'Note to self: revise the spreadsheet for Wednesday's order. Note to Larissa: all casual rosters to be changed to the new format as per meeting please.' Joni and Sarah were still waiting in the doorway. Aaron waved the tape recorder at them. 'Where would I be without this?'

Sarah laughed properly, and Joni wondered if she was on drugs because Kate had said she probably was. But her eyes looked the same as usual, black lines emphasising the hazel. Joni stepped forward.

'Mr Jenson, we're here to submit a petition signed by ...' Joni should have tallied the signatures like Carol told her to. 'By a groundswell of staff. About the smoking break.'

Sarah looked at her bug-eyed. Aaron reached out and Joni handed over the petition. It was strange to see it in his hands. Joni wanted to take it back and leave. Stick it up on the fridge at home and just look at it. All those names. Aaron glanced up.

'Well, thank you, Joni. Leave it with me and I'll —'

'You need to make a copy. For my records,' Joni told him. Sarah was silent now, just staring.

'You haven't made a copy yourself?'

Joni felt her hands start to shake. She folded them behind her back. 'You need to do it,' she told Aaron.

'Kylie isn't here, I'm afraid. You'll have to come back.'

'You need to do it.' Carol had said: *don't leave there without a copy*. That's what the factory people had done with their first petition, and it made all sorts of trouble. Aaron looked with disbelief at Joni, then at Sarah, who smiled. He made a noise and rattled around in a top drawer until he found a card and a key that opened the room next door. They could hear the photocopier.

Sarah leaned towards Joni. 'I went to school with that loser.'

'What?'

'Such a tool. You wouldn't bother talking to him.'

'Does he remember you?'

'Of course he does. He's just pretending not to because.' She gestured around at the office with its IBM and chairs and a bookshelf but no window. Aaron came back and handed Joni the copies. He sat down behind his desk.

'Anything else?'

Joni swallowed. 'You need to review this petition in a timely manner and report back by the next staff meeting.'

'The all-staff is on Friday. It's early because of the public holiday next month —'

'That's correct. We believe a working week is ... good.'

Aaron pursed his lips, looked at the petition again, and nodded. As they closed the door, they could hear him talking to his recorder.

It was too late to have a proper dinner or even a cigarette. Sarah smiled at the Fruit and Veg guy on the way back through and took a couple of bananas right in front of him, which made him laugh. They scoffed them as they put on their aprons. After their shift, Sarah walked Joni to the bus stop so they could debrief over a smoke.

'What are you up to tonight?' Sarah asked.

'I usually just go home. Carol cooks up the rest of the sausages on Fridays for if I want them later.'

'Oh yeah. I might come over. Check out your place. Is Carol your flatmate?'

'My mum.' The lights of the bus appeared down the highway. Sarah stuck out her hand. 'You mean now?'

'Don't you want me to.'

'Yes. I mean.'

Carol was in her chair watching a documentary about hysterectomies. Joni bought most of the food for the house, but Carol could make it stretch. They didn't eat together all that much with Joni's shifts. There was a pile of sausages in the fridge with mashed potatoes and some boiled carrots. Sarah said she'd have some, so Joni made up two plates and put one in the microwave on high for two minutes. In the ad break, Carol twisted in her chair.

'Hi, I'm Sarah.'

Carol looked at Sarah's shirt. 'From the supermarket?'

'Uh huh. I helped Joni with the ... the, you know, the petition thing.'

Carol pressed mute and roused from her chair.

'We'll be quiet,' Joni told her.

'No, no, I want to hear about it.' Carol set her smokes down at the table. Sarah got hers out and waggled the packet.

'Same brand.'

Carol smiled. 'Sandringham girls. Well?'

'It was good. We submitted it.'

'Did you get a copy?'

Joni pulled the photocopied petitions from her bag. Carol stuck her smoke in her mouth and looked at them, grinning. Then she put them on the fridge. 'Look at all those names!'

'Yeah. Joni read management their rights, too. "You better get back to us by Friday", all that.'

'Where's the poster? We'll put that up, too. Just one.' She stepped back to admire the fridge. 'This deserves a drink.' Carol hadn't drunk in years. Joni couldn't even think where they'd have any alcohol in the house, and all the shops were closed. Long walk to get to there anyway. Carol disappeared into the laundry and came back with a dusty bottle of dessert wine.

'It's warm. We'll have to add ice.' Joni and Carol looked at Sarah, who shrugged.

'I'm not fussy.'

Carol gave Sarah the only wine glass and Joni a plastic flute, while she drank hers out of a water glass. They cheers'ed the petition. Carol was glowing after just a few sips. She said that big changes could be made from small houses. Joni told Sarah and Carol about the swan, how you couldn't see its feet working below the muck, so it looked like an elegant black boat sliding through the rubbish. Sarah's eyes shone when she said that. Carol patted Joni's hand.

'There's a lot going on under the surface, isn't there, JJ?'

The three women sat in a circle of smoke until the bottle ran out and the late movie started on the silent TV. At the bus stop Sarah asked Joni if the swan story was real or if it was a metaphor between her and her mum.

'It was real,' Joni said, less sure after the wine.

'Did it flap its wings or anything?'

'No, it just swam along.'

Sarah looked up the highway. Joni had offered for her to

sleep on the couch, but Sarah said she liked the night bus — cold and empty, no one on it. They waved their lighters in front of unlit cigarettes because that was a sure way to make public transport come on time. Sarah put the flame of hers too close and the bus appeared. She took a huge suck and handed it to Joni, laughing out the smoke.

'Fly baby fly!' she shouted. Joni could see her flapping down the empty bus aisle. Plastering herself to the rear window like she'd been squashed there. The Sandringham was unfamiliar on Joni's lips, but it smelled so much like home.

Joni was sure she'd been scheduled to work the coming Friday, but when she looked at the roster she wasn't on it. She asked Charlotte, who said that reasonable changes to the roster were to be expected.

'I was going to apply to attend the Friday meeting. The all-staff.'

'Well now you can definitely attend it. In your own time.'

Quite a few people said they were going to the all-staff — they talked about it in the smoko. Kate was going to give those corporates hell. But the Friday roster was for Charlotte, Holly, and Holly's daughter, who was on school holiday. Only Charlotte was going to the meeting, even though Holly had signed the petition. Joni's bus got in twenty minutes early. She walked through the mall to the supermarket and the quiet Fruit and Veg section, then on to the main staffroom. The door was propped open. Someone was standing in the doorway. Joni tried to excuse herself past, but beyond that person was another and another.

'Hang on, let Joni through,' someone said, and space was made so she could squeeze in. Most of the people had come in on their day off. Even Liv was there, her little daughter trying to climb off her knee. The meeting started with a lot of business that Joni found hard to hear. She concentrated, though, in case they slipped the smoko petition in. She needn't have. As soon as it was mentioned there was a cheer, and everyone who had been jiggling and muttering quietened. Manager Michael had been speaking, then he stepped to one side to introduce Aaron.

'Yeah, morning all. Just a short one to address the petitions around the smoking break.'

'Woo! Smoko!' one of the Fruit and Veg guys called from the back.

Aaron held up seven pieces of paper. Joni thought at first that he'd made copies. Leaning closer, she could see that the other sheets weren't done in Carol's hand but were more of a spreadsheet, with writing and signatures. Carol had said that once you start something, it can build, get bigger, you need to be prepared for that. Someone else had made a save smoko petition, gathered even more names. Joni stepped forwards a little.

'The first petition, submitted by' — Aaron looked at the paper — 'Joni Laing ... is that pronounced *Lang*? Okay ... it calls for smoking breaks to be retained. The other petition, submitted by Charlotte Henley, calls for smoking breaks to be abolished.'

'Skank,' someone whispered.

'On review of both petitions, we have calculated the number of signatures on the first submitted by Laing adds to forty-six, while the number of signatures on the petition submitted by Henley totals seventy-one. Management then reviewed both petitions and decided that, given that the second petition got double the signatures, we find support to abolish the smoking break.'

Everyone started whispering at once. *That's not double, he can't even count. She went and got people from the other stores to sign. I saw her in Wholefoods — she doesn't even shop here.*

Aaron held up his hand. 'But even more than the weight of the signatures, management took the time to explore the discriminatory nature of smoking breaks, which privileges the time of people who smoke more than those who don't. I would like to thank Charlotte, who is working hard out there as the face of the Deli division, for bringing this discriminatory practice to our attention and I'd like to say that this will not be tolerated. Right? Effective immediately.'

The room was silent.

Joni dropped into the Deli after the meeting where Charlotte was pinning up the roster for the week. Joni wasn't scheduled for the weekend double-time and had nothing until Wednesday, a double shift with an awkward hour-and-a-half break in the middle, and then the 6am start on Thursday. Nothing again until the following week.

'Charlotte? What's this?'

Charlotte came back to the board and peered at the sheet. 'Oh, nice. You get a weekend off. And then if you can't do the double, I'm sure the high school girl will, even on her holidays. Keen, that one.'

When she got home, Carol was watching a soap. She hit mute when Joni walked in. 'Did we win?'

Joni shook her head. She couldn't talk for a bit. She set
her bag down on the kitchen chair and got out her packet.
Inhaled. 'There was another petition. They banned smoko.'

'What, the whole lot?' Carol's voice was big but she
stayed in her chair. Joni nodded. She ashed her cigarette into
the clean glass ashtray. Carol watched her.

'Maybe we could do another one?' Joni said.

Carol turned back to the TV. The soap was ending. She
checked the TV guide and changed the channel. 'My show
starts in five,' she said. There was an advertisement for a car.
Carol turned back suddenly with fire in her eyes. Joni leaned
towards the flames. 'Did you get my carton?' Carol asked.

'Oh. I forgot.'

Carol slumped back.

'Have you got enough to last?'

Carol waved her nails and turned up the volume.

Joni started her 6am Wednesday double with not enough
sleep. She had remembered to bring in a small bag of chips
for the morning tea break and took them outside. No
one told her not to smoke and eat. No one said much of
anything. She, Sarah, Charlotte, and the high school kid
were run off their feet all morning. There was a special on
luncheon and twiggy sticks, and they had pork sausages in
stock. Customers came flocking.

At 10:48, with a good hour to go before the lunch
break, Joni took off her apron. Charlotte looked up from
the electronic scales she was reloading with pricing stickers.
'Make your bathroom quick. We're busy.'

Joni reached into her pocket, closed her fingers around

the packet. Her hands weren't shaking when she stuck a Winnie Blue in her mouth. From down by the olives, Sarah started to laugh.

'Don't you *dare*—' Charlotte said, but Joni's lighter was already throwing sparks.

PLAYHOUSE

He was still looking for work. I almost called out, but he left the packed train and boarded another headed for the playhouse. His shows are site specific. You wait in the cold for a woman you instantly hate to wonder out loud about climate change or abortion. I followed him up the escalator — the crown of his head bombed from half a decade of scratching, all devised. At home, he made some of his best work eating apples at the kitchen sink. Now this stride, this determined chin. *As if he's had something done.* The usual cafe was closed, the other one open. He stopped with a view of the electric lines, a plane overhead. Rushing for a comp, I once dropped my sunglasses in a trench just north of here. They were knockoffs but nice. I fully expected to find them while his phone rang out and a pale hand clawed the stage door — laughter, wet hair, mouth working furiously. He lowered his phone to his pocket, and the man at the door saw him. A cover band or a stereo started up somewhere, honestly, 'Love is in the Air'. They both laughed then. And even I felt moved to applaud.

TAKING THE CAT TO HER NEW HOME

The whole place reeks like a cattle truck. That anxious animal smell. The cat keeps to my lap — the space between my stomach and the keyboard — because the flatmate she arrived with has moved out. The other flatmate paces the hall, trying to rent out the vacant room, making enquiries: who wants a middle-aged tabby? I have two more gift card inserts to write before I can do anything about it. One for the foodie and one for the literary lover. For the literary lover, I've rhymed 'poems penned' with 'valentine's friend'.

'They won't use "valentine's friend",' I tell the cat. 'Too ambiguous.' Her ear rotates towards me, then to the door. The other flatmate appears with two wax boxes.

'You do it. She likes you.' He sets them on the floor. The dish inside one of them has spilled, dribbling milk out the hole. The cat is a dead weight until I put her inside, then the whole thing arcs, quivers. Her eye at the hole.

'Maybe ...'

'What?' The flatmate is sweating. He really has organised

this whole thing.

'Well, she *likes* me.'

He whines. 'This woman already said she'd take her —'

I hold up my hands. Watch him struggle the box back out into the hall. And I'm familiar with all of it — the hollow hiss in the murk. The piles of fur.

GUNFLOWER

When we finally arrived in Georgia, I picked a fight with Rick over the grim double motel room he'd booked on the very edge of a spit that services fishermen and boating enthusiasts who don't care where they sleep, just as long as they can get out on the water. Rick would stay there for a few days to work at the wobbly table. He'd eat burgers from the diner. There was a battered copy of *The Ultimate Saltwater Fishing Guide* next to the Bible in the bedside table drawer. But he was right: it was the perfect place. No one cared who went in or out, as long as we paid in advance.

'Will you be able to get any work done?' I asked as we climbed into the lumpy motel bed — he on the right-hand side, me on the left. He was trying to edit a shared document on the tenuous wi-fi. I repeated my question.

'I'll try.'

'Would you be this worried if I was just going to a clinic for a script?'

'I don't know, Joan. That's not exactly an option. And anyway, I've never done anything like this.'

From the window, I couldn't make out the lights of the *RV Gerda Faal*, the ship that supposedly waited for us, twelve nautical miles off the spit. I watched the car lights on the curtains instead — late fishers turning in for the night — and thought about who Rick might have unknowingly impregnated in his twenties, before we met. Women who might have terminated in their hometown when it was safe and easy to do so — through their doctor or buying pills online. Who hadn't decided to haul-arse over three nauseatingly hot states to flag down a passing abortion ship.

'Come back,' Rick called. He had fallen asleep with his laptop on his chest. My breasts throbbed as I climbed in beside him. He put his hand on my stomach as if protecting the very thing we were trying to be rid of.

By morning I had a cricked neck and a stress stye, swollen, baboon-like in my eyelid. Something in the air — maybe dust mites in the hotel — was setting my sinuses off, too.

I told Rick, 'I thought sea air was supposed to be good for you?' Maybe it sounded accusing because he left, closing the door very quietly behind him. I watched out the window for the ship. The *Gerda Faal* — *GF* — was dubbed 'Your Girlfriend', 'the feminazi ship of death'; its services 'floating acts of terrorism'. Through all the broken condoms and forgotten contraceptive pills I had never in my forty-four years become knowingly pregnant, so in my head I called it 'The Good Ship Abortion'. Whatever the name, the ship floated into my orbit just in time.

•

Down at the diner, fresh coffee dripped through the machine, but there was no one to serve it. I 'um, hello'ed through reception and then came back around to stare at the shredded cheese, deli slices, pimentos, mayonnaise, and bread all set out behind the glass. There was a metallic taste on my tongue that wouldn't wash out, and I was nauseous with or without food. Inside me, matter was pulling together, becoming nuclear in my gut. This must be how scientists feel, I thought, when they look out at space and realise that life is possible. I found myself behind the counter shoving a slice of bread in my mouth to calm the gnawing hunger, then fixed a pretty nice meal out of the cabinet food, leaving a bunch of notes by the till. No one came to tell me not to. Back in the room I said to Rick, 'You really need to eat, hun. Here: sandwiches.' Because he was pale as anything when he returned.

'Listen, how illegal is this thing?'

'The ship is anchored internationally so it operates under the laws of its own flag.' I tried the sandwich, put it back down. 'And obviously maritime law. If you think about it —'

'You can still get surgery right here, only a few states away, Joan.' He pointed north. 'Forget this.'

I had used a similar ship, the now decommissioned *AWB: Abortions Without Borders*, as one of the case studies for a unit on activism in my Ethics and the Law class. 'What,' I asked my students, 'are the legal requirements for a ship performing abortions in international waters? And how far can and should such an actor go in order to fulfil their mandate?'

'How much of your body do you need to put on the line to prove a point?' Rick asked me now. He wanted to drive to Illinois and get it done. I wanted him to see that the very act of seeking abortion services from a ship showed how desperate the situation had become. My old law-school buddies were building a case, I told him. A partnered middle-aged white woman, seven-and-a-half weeks pregnant and willing to document? I was gold.

'A guinea pig is what you are.' He peered out the window.

'What are you looking at?'

He moved the curtain to show me. Nothing outside. No one. Not a car or a boat.

'It's because they all got up so early,' I insisted, 'and that's good for us: if we can get to our charter without having to explain.'

'We could just leave,' he said again. 'Take the coast route and be in Springfield or New Jersey by tomorrow.'

'We always said we'd *do* something.' I was yelling suddenly, but that had been happening of late. The hormones made me edgeless. 'We always said that. Change needs to happen at a seismic level. Well, this is it, Rick.'

He had no patience for yelling and turned back to the bright road, the light cast off the sea.

'Yes, but a fucking ship?'

I got dressed in a very specific way, according to the instructions sent through — a black singlet and black leggings over dark underwear. A khaki sundress and a warm jacket over the top. In my day pack were a set of tightly rolled sweats, changes of underwear, my phone charger, pens, a toothbrush, toothpaste, and a small tube of moisturiser. Essentials for a few days without being conspicuous. I added case printouts and my laptop, which contained my Ethics and the Law marking for the semester. The last of it, in fact: my subject had been axed. Rick buried his face in his computer, trying to catch up on work, while I shoved tissues and antihistamines in a side pocket and asked him if he would like me to pack the fishing book to read on the boat. He nodded, miserable. We would go together to the port, and he would accompany me on the charter, but he wouldn't be allowed on *Gerda Faal*, where only pregnant people could be passengers unless they were under sixteen. I took a strange solace in observing his discomfort; his fate decided by others.

Nearing the harbour, we saw one other person. They put their hand to their forehead as though against a spotlight and gazed at us as we drove by. This piqued Rick's paranoia enough to circle around twice before he was satisfied that the man was gone, the streets desolate. Instead of pulling up in the empty parking lot, we parked on the street, shouldering our backpacks and cutting over a concrete barrier to walk along the wet grey sand. Our feet made ghost-shaped puddles, until the water sucked away, leaving no trace.

'*In your times of sadness and grief, you saw only one set of footprints, but it was then that I carried you.*' I told Rick, who sniggered. 'I reckon there'd be marks from where Jesus picked me up to carry me through my hardship. And wouldn't his imprints be so much deeper with the weight of lifting me over the sand?'

'And I say, for a brilliant person — *with a law degree*, as if we could forget — you're still pretty into that Bible shit.'

•

When I was eight, I saw a vision. We were in Dallas so Dad could interview for a job he didn't get, and my little sister and I were excited to stay in a hotel on the sixth floor. It was foggy, and from the window I saw the mists clear and a cross appear through the clouds. I knew it was God. I told my parents in the elevator on the way to the buffet. They were thrilled that their bookish daughter was showing an interest in her Adventist upbringing, and for a time I followed them willingly to church. When I was a teenager, my conviction shifted to other pursuits. High on the football field with friends from choir, I talked in whispered terms about the cross and my friends shared their encounters, conversions, rejections. If the nuances of being a practising Christian were a little lost on me, the cross was not. I could still picture the shape of it rising above the cloud — a grim cut of stone with a circle through the middle. Years later, Rick and I looked the cross up online to discover it was likely the top of a church sticking up through fog. I was embarrassed for myself and for my parents. How easily they had accepted a child's vision, or version, of God. How they now voted with that same readiness — believing whoever told them what they wanted to hear.

The dock was empty but for two boats, one of them the *Sea Maiden* — a cruiser boat-for-hire that would transport us to the *Gerda Faal*. Later, I would remember the skipper's stretched smile welcoming us like a honeymooning couple on their second marriage. In the moment, though, I was just relieved to see the skipper in the otherwise empty dock and to climb aboard, finding a cushioned seat on the clean boat. The diner sandwich sat unhappily in me. I worried about the long journey into deep waters. My stye felt like it took up my entire face and my nose dripped constantly. The skipper handed us each a glass of sparkling wine and took a photo. Somewhere on Rick's phone is a picture of this moment, of us smiling as hard as we could while we clinked glasses. We had been warned that this bit of coast could be treacherous in bad weather. But despite black clouds gathering in the east, the trip out was lovely. In the midday light, land blew away from us like smoke leaving a mouth. The water widened. When I closed my eyes, the horizon was painted on the back of my eyelids. The blasts of wind — alternating warm and cold currents — soothed my stomach. Rick came to sit by me and touched my arm.

'Are you okay?'

I told him I needed to keep facing forwards or I'd throw up.

'Oh.' He looked embarrassed, and I envied him his not-pregnant body.

'There,' said the skipper. Two hours and fifteen minutes after we left the dock, we passed into international waters. The waves had picked up and the sun was doing that thing where it bursts brightly through black clouds, making everything seem overly dramatic. The abortion ship looked small on the sea. As we drew closer the vessel grew to the 140-metre, 9300 -tonne former merchant liner it was — a small feeder on a pro bono ten-year lease through an anonymous donor. The

letters that spelled out *Gerda Faal* in bright blue on the side
of the black ship would once have been elegant. Now there
was a yellow slash through the middle, the word *Gunflower*
spraypainted above. The Nordic Cross of Iceland's national
flag flapped on the mast. I leaned over to tell Rick that
Iceland had one of the most liberal abortion-on-demand
laws in the world, available up to twenty-two weeks.

He replied, 'Some of the states back there have liberal
-enough abortion laws, too. Just saying.' But I could tell he
was interested — he loved a fact.

I scanned the wind-blasted deck as we pulled up
alongside but saw no one. Then our radio blared.

'*Sea Maiden* this is *GF*, over.'

'I read you, *Gerda Faal*,' the skipper responded. He gave
me a wink, which wasn't reassuring. I gripped Rick's hand.

'*Sea Maiden*, are you in trouble? You've come alongside
very close.'

'Yes, ah … *Gerda Faal* … we've run out of fuel.'

'Please confirm, is it a fuel leak?'

'No, *Gerda Faal,* I didn't fuel up properly. My fault.'

'Confirming that this is not a fuel leak and that you are
in need of fuel.'

'Roger that, *Gerda Faal*.'

'*Sea Maiden*, can you wait for a ship of your flag to
assist?'

'Negative, *Gerda Faal*. I have US citizens on board who
need to return. I've strayed out of US waters. I know this is
unorthodox, *Gerda Faal*, but I need your help.'

A pause. I was so totally engaged with this version of
events that I almost forgot why we were there.

'*Sea Maiden*, confirming that it's our obligation to assist.

Confirming that we have a tank of fuel. Confirming that we will send a crew member to deliver this to you.'

This was the sign that I should peel off my coat and sundress to the strange ballet costume underneath. A crew member wearing the same appeared at the railing of the *Gerda Faal*, while the skipper of the *Sea Maiden* instructed me to stand so the other person could climb down in front of me. For a moment we were touching, twins in our strange unitards, before she handed me an empty jerry can to pass to the skipper and slipped past me into the water. Now I was her. Observers might be fooled into thinking that another person hadn't boarded the ship. In all the kerfuffle, there was no time to say goodbye to Rick, no time to even turn around before the skipper had handed over my backpack and sent me up the ladder.

Nigerian second mate and communications manager, Fa'iqah, pulled me up the final rung.

'Welcome to *Gunflower*,' she said and asked me to wait a moment, disappearing through a heavy door. I was left alone on the black-painted deck, the *Sea Maiden* speeding away, Rick craning past my desperately waving hand, my whole world unsteady. This wasn't a fake day trip on the *Gerda Faal* anymore. It was a strange, dark ship, and I was on it, ill at the very thought of doing anything other than hiding in bed for the next six months, despite the lifelong consequences. Fa'iqah appeared again, steady at my elbow along the swaying deck.

'I always wanted to live there,' she said, gazing portside. 'I thought it sounded so great, you know?'

'It does sound great.'

She guided me through another thick door and down a

set of stairs. A cabin with a single bed tucked in the corner, a separate bathroom, and a round porthole.

'You missed lunch, but Chef made this up for you.' I couldn't even look at the sandwiches. 'Or maybe a peppermint tea.' She turned back the cover on the bed. 'Here, Joan. Lie down. I'll call you later to meet the crew.'

She left. I fiddled with the hefty painted handle to the porthole, hoping to wave again out the window, but the *Sea Maiden* was well gone, and I was alone in a place called Gunflower. I felt the swell change under the boat, increasing the great, steady heartbeat of the ship. Being there was like being in the stomach of a whale. I was Jonah, inside something very alive — both strong and fragile. I tried Rick's phone, but we were both out of range. Sent him a series of failed pictures — my blotchy face, the room. The first few hours were a cocktail dream of morning sickness and sea sickness, antihistamines, and drops to treat my stye. The pregnancy pinned me to the swaying bed. My left breast, especially, aching. I turned my face to the pillow and bawled. When I closed my eyes, I saw bright ocean and a gargantuan humpback whale rising out of it. It slammed down on the surface, its mouth massive. The internal phone rang.

'I never thought we'd be working around here, in US waters,' Marg, the burly Icelandic chief engineer and first mate, said in the control room at the top of the bridge. 'None of us did. We didn't think we'd be needed. Pretty naïve.' In her fifties, with short grey hair, Marg's legs were splayed, a casual arm over a bolted chair to keep balance. The crew assembled, brewing coffee, handing out cookies, and waiting for their captain to arrive. They were friendly — the younger women reminded me of my students — but I sensed wariness. I felt hungover and also in need of a drink. I felt too old to be carrying a fetus and also like a teenager rebelling. I needed a mother, a sister at least. I followed Marg around the room while she did introductions, trying to mimic her oceanic sway. Elena, the British communications coordinator and deck crew, and Sandy, the anaesthetist and nurse from Delhi — both in their twenties; Alek, the Polish Icelandic communications officer and assistant nurse in her late thirties, who had been my body double in the black jumpsuit, braving the waters to get me aboard. English was their common language, with a smattering of French and, occasionally, what I assumed was a Nordic swear word. I bumped painfully into the map table.

'Why does it say "Gunflower" on the side of the ship?' I asked and Elena laughed, pointing at Alek.

'She did it. Poor old Gerda Faal, whoever she was.'

'A goddess, wasn't she?' said Sandy. 'Gerda?'

'I don't know,' said Alek. 'But Gunflower makes more sense.'

'Sure.' Marg leaned her elbows on the map table. 'Gun — the old Norse for war — and flower, obviously, the seed part of the plant, its reproductive organs. Birth and death.'

I took a bite of a ginger cookie.

'They're not homemade,' Mina, the ship's older Pakistani British chef and safety officer, warned. 'I do three cooked meals a day though. For when you feel like eating.' Captain Hannah Durand arrived, and a certain calm settled over the room. Her face was weathered; she had the bright, sparking black eyes of someone capable of holding many things at once.

'Sorry about these salty sea dogs,' she said to me, appraising the crew. 'Have they made any sense? We haven't seen other people in weeks.'

Hannah was late because of the cleaning, rubbish removal, ship maintenance, and safety checks they all took it in turns to do.

'What's my job?' I asked, trying to ignore the nausea of the swaying horizon.

'You're the patient,' Hannah said, suddenly serious. 'Patient number one. Here to remind the United States that these pills are safer than penicillin.'

I was supposed to have the abortion pill at 1600 and stay on the ship for one night for observation, but there was a complication. Elena and Alek were having trouble getting through to the lawyers to confirm the go-ahead.

'It's not a deal breaker,' Hannah told me. 'There have been plenty of hostile countries where we haven't been able to touch base with land crew — but we're treading carefully with the US law team in terms of liability. It's new territory.'

Hey, I wrote to Rick on the ship's creaking shipmail system, acutely aware that the account was shared by the whole crew. *We might need a backup plan.* My subtext: I'm still pregnant here, where are you?

Back in my small, swaying cabin I suddenly recalled, with great clarity, the look on Rick's face when I came out with the wet stick and the two pink lines. His quiet devastation while I raved. The timing! Right when my university course — beloved to the few who enrolled — was cancelled. Instead, they needed tutors in property law. 'We don't even own property!' I yelled. Couldn't my fertility have surged when there were still rulings to protect it? It was punishment.

'Watch out, your Bible is showing,' Rick muttered, and we laughed like our faces would fall off.

Where was Rick now? Eating fries at the diner? Lying diagonal across the double bed? I'd climbed the ship's ladder, yes, but I couldn't help feeling abandoned. These strangers, and this strange body that was growing something so powerful that its very existence divided nations, drove people to harm themselves and turn against their loved ones. At the same time, I felt kinship with these women. They had braved a hostile international crossing and worse political climate to help people like me. There was a buzz between them, as well as the ease necessary for a crew who lived in one another's pockets for months on end. They grinned in the stairwell that connected the decks while we waited for the directive.

'Hey, it's our favourite patient,' Marg said when I arrived in the mess room for a meal.

I managed a smile. 'Your *only* patient.'

For dinner, I took clear soup because the swells and morning (noon and night) sickness were doing all the bad things to my guts. I got myself outside to gulp in air that carried tendrils of an Atlantic chill, then wandered the decks, trying to calm my nerves for the days ahead.

I woke in the early hours feeling oddly normal. The nausea was gone, along with the panicky butterfly feeling, the strange pressure on my stomach. I was sure I wasn't pregnant anymore. The thought got me up and searching for Captain Hannah, who was on shift. At night, the bridge was plunged into darkness, with only the radar lights and the occasional wink of another ship on a desolate peak of wave for company. Hannah beckoned me, and I felt my way towards the giant dashboard.

'I might not need it,' I told her. 'I'm sorry. I know you were counting on me.' Hannah whistled a tune through her teeth and took my temperature with a kit from a fanny pack, asked if I was bleeding.

'They often feel better at night,' she said, zipping her pack.

'Who?'

'Our patients.' I felt, then, the presence of the thousands of women, from the Philippines to Madagascar, who had passed through the ship's services. 'You're likely still pregnant,' Hannah went on. 'We'll do another test before the procedure anyway, and if it's positive we'll continue as planned, whether we hear from those lawyers or not.'

'And if I'm not pregnant?'

'There's always another woman who needs an abortion, Joan. Two hundred thousand, actually. And that's just today.'

I felt a sudden shame. Hannah continued to whistle her unrecognisable tune until her puff ran out. She laughed. 'I'm the only one who would get away with this whistling onboard: it's bad luck. But then, women on ships at all are supposed to be bad luck.' She flicked a switch and made a note on an iPad. 'There are lots of advantages to being captain, actually. The big cabin, the best hate mail, the queen shift — that's what we're on now. 8pm to 12am is the shift of lost youth; 12am to 4am is the dog shift — it's fucking awful — and 4am to 8am is queen shift. After it, I get a big breakfast with anyone onboard.' She was trying to make me feel better.

'I guess we're alone otherwise,' I managed to contribute.

'Right. We eat together, like family.'

'Why couldn't Rick come on the ship?' I'd already asked my old lawyer friends in their careful suits. Their answer: insurance.

'Just one patient on board is rare,' Hannah said instead. 'It's usually twenty or more a day. One port in Poland, where Alek joined us, we had a hundred coming through. It was nuts. It's not just that there isn't room for extras.' She leaned towards me, her face mottled in the dark. 'Some patients have conceived through rape or incest, or they're escaping violence. They're frightened. We've had a couple of men with wombs on here who were pregnant, too, and nonbinary people. It's just easier if there aren't cis men onboard.'

A wind picked up and drummed at the doors. A tiredness I'd only known in the last few weeks dragged at me, but I wasn't ready for my cabin — both a protective cocoon and prison.

'I guess I'm still pregnant.' My voice cracking, masculine.

'It's going to be alright,' Hannah said. 'It's an easy, non-surgical procedure with only a day or two recovery.'

'But do I really need this? I've got Rick ...' I pointed in the direction of where I thought Rick might be. Out there.

'Well, that's the thing about reproductive rights,' Hannah said grimly into our black surrounds. 'They don't discriminate. Or they're not supposed to. They're for everybody, no matter how they've conceived.' Even so, I thought, on my way back down to my cabin. Those children who had survived rape. No access to abortion could mean the end of their lives, rather than the redirection effect it would have on mine.

●

If I felt okay in the night, by morning I was someone beaten. The six flights of stairs, the constant bracing, the nausea, wobbling side to side, the flying around in bed, the worry: *what if something goes wrong and I can't take the pill? What if nothing goes wrong and I can?* Through every window, the sketched blue of the ocean, the grey smear of the sky. The water was 2.5 miles deep and swirled against a bow travelling at 18 knots. While my world bloated, the crew kept busy at their seaworthy tasks: hauling trunk-sized rope across the salty deck, welding small bits of metal to larger bits of metal, plotting courses on the bridge. The internal phone rang again. My task was to make my way to one of the three temperature-controlled containers that had been converted into a surgery, supplies storage, and recovery room. No word from the lawyers, but as we remained in international waters, I consented to go ahead — I wanted to have the case study ready for when we made contact. Also, I needed an abortion. In the surgery, Sandy handed me a pregnancy test. I went to the attached bathroom and watched the pink lines practically pop off the stick in confirmation. Alek swiped on the video to document our coordinates throughout the procedure — proof that we weren't breaking US law.

The pills had storybook names, mifepristone and misoprostol — the good witches of the east. They should have come as a magnificent green paste delivered by a woman wearing bells and amulets. The actual pill was so white and unassuming in Sandy's gloved palm I worried that she was giving me ibuprofen.

'Mifepristone,' she confirmed. I swallowed it with a glass

of fresh water from the ship's water-regeneration system — it tasted like a void, the salt (and nutrients) sucked out of it. Mifepristone prevents the growth of the fetus. The second, misoprostol, would cause uterine contractions. I lay down on one of the gurneys in the clinic for thirty minutes of observation. My mind flung back to my homeland, where in some states they were arresting women for taking these very pills. I heard the thrum of another motor and sat up, heart pounding.

'It's just the generator,' Sandy told me, though she went to the door to check — a blast of salty air through the surgical space. She gave me a real ibuprofen and a dissolvable anti-nausea pill.

'You're doing well, Joan. You can head back. Read through the fact sheet.' She handed me a printout which swam in my vision. 'Let me know if you have questions.'

'Will it hurt?'

'There'll be cramping, nausea.'

'So I just ...?'

'You wait. We're right here with you, for whatever you need. Try to rest.'

Elena and Alek had set up my room with a hot water bottle, maternity pads, old magazines from a dizzying array of countries, and a small DVD player with a flip-up screen and a selection of films from *All That Jazz* to *A Star is Born* to, hilariously, *Free Willy*. Not a careful curation: *Three Men and a Baby* was in there without a case. I pulled my old printouts from my backpack, heavily underlined and marked up. I could quote by heart the moment when, in 1974, Sarah Weddington, the lawyer successful for Roe, said, 'No one can say here is the dividing line, here is where life begins, here is

... life is here and life is not over here.' And, 'We are here to advocate that the decision as to whether or not a particular woman will continue to carry or will terminate a pregnancy is a decision that should be made by that individual.' The 2022 overturning remained a frightening read. I often stumbled over it mid-lecture to young law students. 'By the time the Fourteenth Amendment was adopted, three quarters of the States had made abortion a crime at any stage of pregnancy. This consensus endured until the day Roe was decided. Roe either ignored or misstated this history, and Casey declined to reconsider Roe's faulty historical analysis.' The weight of it pushed me back to the bed.

After an hour, Sandy called in to check my progress. I reported a pressure in my abdomen and a sore lower back, but I couldn't quite describe the rest. The anxiety of being all at sea in my body and in the Constitution that was my country's real religion.

'Can I use the email?' I asked.

'Yes, but take it easy on the stairs. You have your pad in?'

On the bridge, Hannah was trying the skipper of the *Sea Maiden*, with no response.

'No contact for twelve hours,' she said, then noticed me. 'Feeling okay?' I nodded. I didn't want to be sent back down. Amid the many emails from people seeking help around the world, there was one from Rick from the night before. He'd been spending his time in the motel plotting alternatives. A doctor cousin in upstate New York he hadn't seen since he was a kid. Our friends in California. An elaborate system of international postage that involved my anxious sister setting up a PO box and running abortion pills over borders. I hung on his scattered practicality.

'Don't worry, babe, it's done,' I wrote back. 'The eagle has flown.'

The cramping started after two hours. I made it back down to the cabin with Sandy beside me. She refilled the hot water bottle and placed a kettle in my room. I took another ibuprofen and put on a documentary about historic buildings of Denmark, then tried Rick's copy of *The Ultimate Saltwater Fishing Guide*. Neither was absorbing. The cramping became more intense. When I went into the bathroom to change my pad, there was a clot the size of a walnut. I called Sandy and, while I waited for her, the pain got worse. Hannah arrived instead and took my temperature again.

'A little high but that's normal, you're doing well. Keep resting. You're in for a few hours yet.'

It was like the worst period cramps I've ever had combined with food poisoning. I vomited into the cabin sink, then leaned in the shower with the hot water over my belly — realising that it was empty now, or emptying. Brushed my teeth. Another anti-nausea pill and another ibuprofen. To look out a porthole was to see green vomit on the stomach's horizon. The kettle boiled and I carefully filled the bottle, leaning against the wall to combat the slow swaying, the bursts of pain. I found the least uncomfortable position in the bed, a pillow between my knees, heat on my stomach, and dozed with the fishing book open near my face. Sandy visited twice more and put a cool hand to my forehead. I wanted to cry at the childish familiarity of being looked after. Wondered if I should have contacted my mother. Who would have been horrified with every aspect, from the reminder that Rick and I weren't married, to the abortion, to floating around on some strange ship like a pirate. I closed my eyes again and listened to the chandelier sound of water tinkling against the ship's hull.

I managed the cramps with painkillers through the first day and they were milder by the second. I was still bleeding, though, and wearing a giant pad, gingerly navigating the rocking stairwells. Mina served up minestrone with chunky homemade bread that we ate in the easy company of Fa'iqua, Sandy, and Elena. With no contact from the *Sea Maiden* for twenty-four hours, Hannah gave the go-ahead to track west towards the meeting point anyway, just beyond US territorial waters. We arrived at 1351 — a few minutes ahead of time. No sign of the *Sea Maiden*. The swathe of emails I had previously scrolled through to get to Rick's had all been opened and responded to by the comms team — there were no new ones. I opened the last, marked yesterday, though it was supremely confidential. It was from a patient in Louisiana, seeking help.

'I think the shipmail is out,' I called over the noise of the control room. 'Have you been getting any messages?'

Marg came to lean over me.

'Nothing since yesterday. That's weird.' She went down to the engine room to reboot the modem. Hannah tried to contact the *Sea Maiden* again on the two-way but got no response.

'Are all our comms down?' she asked Marg when she came back in.

'I've rebooted, and I can't see any problem. But messages aren't coming through.'

'We'll have to wait, then. There's no problem with us anchoring here. You're within the law, Joan,' Hannah reassured me. 'This is why we do these test runs. It may be ... Marg? It may be that *Sea Maiden* isn't suitable and that this port isn't either. Can we look at other options?'

New Orleans or Florida, though Georgia had been chosen because of its broad access to the Atlantic — further north, and *Gunflower*'s services in pro-choice states weren't needed; further south, and the Gulf of Mexico got tricky. On the email, the same message from the same woman asking for help. She would have been one day further into her pregnancy. One day closer to the time where it would become difficult to abort, another day closer to the place where she wouldn't be able to do it at all. I felt a sudden emptiness, a surge of anxiety, but also the restoration of myself.

Back down in my cabin, my phone was still out of range. I fully expected to hear activity outside at any moment — coast guards, military, the *Sea Maiden* — but there were only sea birds who had ventured far enough to check out our vessel in hopes of fishy debris. I noticed when they, too, fell silent and there was only the engine, the water sloshing past. When the intercom blared, I knocked my elbow painfully on the porthole handle.

'Prepare to enter US territorial waters,' Hannah said and hung up. I got myself back up the stairs. They were all business there. The air crackled. On the bridge, Fa'iqah and Hannah had changed into their white shirts with stripes. They cradled walkie-talkies like violins. These women who must have docked a hundred times together never took their eyes off the sea. While everyone rushed starboard, watching the water, I got the urge to grab the handle that controlled the speed and to push it through slow, medium, to fast. I wanted to go home. Hannah returned, lips pressed. Eyes scanning. She motioned for the binoculars and peered out again, then placed them back on the giant dashboard.

'Is it a public holiday? A strike?'

I realised she was talking to me. I wasn't entirely sure what day it was.

'No other vessels.' She bent over the radar and her frown deepened. 'Shit.' Picked up the internal phone. 'Marg, the radar is out, too. I'm not kidding ... Well, you come back up and look at it then ... No, this is more important.' Marg entered, panting. 'I can't see anything, can you?' Hannah looked at her like she might laugh. 'Where's the land?' Marg shook her head. 'Is this some military thing? Can they do that?' Hannah turned to me again — the American attaché. I tilted my head in what I hoped was a solid maybe. Our military definitely had the power and the will to spend time and money jamming all the communications of one little ship. Hannah, Fa'iqah, and Marg stood in silence for a moment, then began rolling out charts. Mapping A — where we were — to B, the land the radar wasn't recognising: North America; the tidal flow — A to C; then the water track — C to D — which was the true course to steer. My womb continued its dull clunk, thunder receding. Hannah handed me a set of binoculars. 'Report anything: fog, birds, other boats. Whatever you see.' I was glad to have something to do. We cruised at low speed towards our destination again. They couldn't rely on the radar, so we each aimed our gaze south-west, looking for Jacksonville. I hallucinated objects wriggling in and out of my vision and reported this until Fa'iqah showed me how to adjust the binoculars. Then I couldn't see anything of note. Hannah and Marg were consulting again — both the defunct radar and their maps.

'But where is it?'

'Where's what?' I asked.

'America.'

Marg believed that walking around was good for cramping, and Hannah didn't dispute it, so I followed Marg down to the engine room, its oily lack of air. Three days ago, this would have made me ill. Now I perched gingerly on a plastic crate and watched Marg send out a warning over the speaker system, hit an alarm. There was a millionth of a second of darkness before the orange glow of the safety lights seeped over us. Marg used the walkie-talkie to confirm again with the bridge, then rebooted the system. This would take around thirty seconds, she explained, and we waited in the relative silence left by the lack of engine roar, the water muttering around the keel.

'Are we below the water level now?'

'We are,' she said. 'Deep in the beast.' She asked me if I'd read *Moby Dick*. I hadn't. She hadn't either but said she often thought about it in moments like these.

'I spend all my time down here,' she said. 'I don't see much of the patients. So when the engine is out or getting restarted

I realise what we are: a tin can floating on a powerful entity with little control.' She gave a squeak when, right at that moment, the system came back to life.

'All systems go,' Marg told Hannah.

A pause. 'Not exactly. The radar is still out.'

There was no choice but to use an emergency beacon. This was Hannah's final and least-favoured option.

'It's the message it sends. A ship full of women doing abortions. Putting out this beacon ... it's admitting failure. But what else are we going to do?'

'We've tried everything within reason,' Marg said.

Hannah's eyes flashed. 'Is there anything, you know, beyond reason ...?'

'Besides just ploughing into the United States without any correspondence.'

'Yes,' said Hannah.

'Yes, *what*?

'Yes, let's try that. Our communication is down. What else are we supposed to do?'

'Send out the emergency —'

'That's the last option. We haven't tried this yet.'

We surged on and on. The crew listless. Exhausted from pulling long shifts and watching the eerily calm horizon in case we suddenly bumped into unplotted land. Hannah cross-checked the charts; Marg looked angry. They both glared at the sea.

'Well, it must be wrong,' Marg told her.

'You look then. You look and tell me what's wrong.'

What was wrong was that the United States of America — the whole coast of Georgia specifically — should have formed our entire horizon by now. Part of me was sure I'd spot it. But the only thing visible ahead, with the naked eye or through the binoculars, was ocean. The waves had died down, and the water sparkled as one endless sheet of blue. I found myself panting, staring out in disbelief with the crew.

'So we confirm that, one: we have no comms or digital navigation,' Hannah began, her voice so tired it was robotic. 'Two: we are lost. Three: we've lost contact with our target country, the United States, and our flag country, Iceland. We don't know whose territorial waters we're straying into.'

I asked if that was dangerous.

'Extremely. Iceland is a neutral flag, but we're unaware of the international situation. Anything could have happened. Something *has* happened.' The crew was silent. 'Theories?'

'Okay.' Alek took us all in. 'Maybe the US got blown up.' I let out a snort but no one else was laughing.

'Maybe,' said Hannah. 'But where's the explosion? Where's the smoke or debris? We were only twelve from land when we lost contact. It's unlikely. And?'

'We were hacked,' Fa'iqah put in. 'I think that's the most likely option. I'd say we're ...' Fa'iqah looked outside again at that calm, calm sea. 'We're just doing circles. And if we head west, we'll hit land.'

'We did head west. We are west. There's nothing here.'

'We've cruised down past Cuba then. We're in the Caribbean.'

Hannah nodded. 'That does seem possible. Good theory. Anything else?'

Elena raised her hand. 'We're dead.'

'What?'

'We died. And this is limbo. Purgatory. We're floating between times.'

'Do I look dead to you?'

'You do look a bit half-dead.'

Hannah laughed hoarsely. 'I feel a little bit dead.'

'You need some sleep.'

'Does everyone agree to work with Fa'iqah's theory for now? Keep going ahead and expect to encounter the Caribbean islands, or at least the Dominican Republic or Venezuela if we're facing that way?'

So we're just going to South America now? I wanted to yell. *That's your plan?* But I was frozen by the realisation that we'd be lucky to end up there.

'Roger that,' Marg said to Hannah. 'Sleep. We'll wake you if something happens.'

When Hannah moved her hip popped. She propped open the bridge door. 'All those women,' she said. I realised she was looking at me. 'They were waiting for us. How many?'

Elena shook her head. 'Once word was out, it was already hundreds. If we'd been able to promote ourselves properly, thousands.'

Hannah sucked a breath as shaky as I felt.

I woke only an hour later and went to find crackers and peanut butter in the empty kitchen. My phone was still out of range. It had been over a day since we last had contact with the outside world. Up on the bridge, Fa'iqah was trying to chart her way out.

'Even if we were right in the middle of the Atlantic,' she was saying to Marg, pointing at the map, which now detailed two different courses, depending on where we might possibly be, 'we would have come into signal or encountered other vessels by now.'

'There're no seabirds,' I said.

'None,' said Marg.

'What about fish?'

She pulled me into a sudden hug. 'Genius! A fish can tell us a lot.'

I'd been fishing twice in my life — the last time with Rick, six years ago on the Little Missouri river, where we caught a gasping trout — and I'd never seen a deep-sea fishing rod. I retrieved Rick's book from my cabin and flipped through the pages until I found the classes of rod that matched a well-worn blue in a storage cupboard. There were frozen sardines in the kitchen freezer to soak in warm water. Back on deck, I gingerly hooked a little fish and dropped the line.

I was glaring at the hairline horizon, willing for land, whales, or ships, when the line jerked brutally, and I hauled a living being out of the water. Its silver fins seemed shark-like, and it was huge on the deck. Marg came down to peer at it.

'It's an albacore,' I informed her, Rick's book open.

'It's a tuna. You used a good rod for that.' I looked through the book again. It was a tuna. 'Anyway, it bumps out one theory,' Marg said.

'Where are we then?'

Marg shrugged. 'Tuna are everywhere. They're in Iceland. They're in Mexico. They're in Australia. And there's different types. That book will tell you ... No, what I mean is that at least it proves we're not dead.'

'In what way?'

'How can there be fish if we're dead?'

'But the *fish* is dead.'

We gazed down at it, the blood on the deck.

My fish made it into a curry, along with other fish from the freezer. We gathered in the dining room to make our way through the ship's supply of wine — an attempt to improve the mood.

Alek leaned towards me. 'So, when you went fishing today, did you get a sense of the bottom?'

'The ocean floor?' If we were still in deep sea, that was 2.5 miles down.

Alek sipped her wine from a coffee mug. 'I figure if the land has disappeared, the sea floor has, too. That we're bottomless.'

Hannah pushed her plate away and ordered the second captain and engineer up to the bridge. The rest of us watched them leave. I had the overwhelming sense that everything that was solid and sure might disappear if I took my eye off it.

'There's another theory,' Elena said once the door slammed shut. 'Two, actually.'

'Other than we've all died? That there's nothing beneath us?' I asked. I was still watching the door, willing Hannah to heave back through it with a plan.

'That we're mad. Collectively.'

That seemed plausible. 'And the other?'

'That we're in the Bermuda Triangle. Actually, that's my working theory.'

Dinner was cleared, the kitchen cleaned, and the doors to the cabins along the crew deck propped open — easy in the calm weather. No one wanted to be alone. The crew didn't look dead or whatever qualifies as collectively psychotic, just wired, watchful of anyone going past in case of news. I paced the halls. In the final cabin, Sandy was whistling.

'How are you feeling?' she asked when she saw me.

'Better. You're whistling. Isn't that bad luck?'

'Totally. It calls the bad winds,' she said, then pursed her lips again.

'But *you're* whistling.'

'A storm indicates change in the pressure system, which means that we're somewhere, not nowhere. Where there's a storm, there's something.'

I asked if I could try it, too, and, after some tuneless blowing, we both settled on an approximation of happy birthday. A couple of the others emerged to join in, until Alek told us to shut it.

'It's annoying. And calling up the winds is nothing to mess with.'

I phoned from my cabin to the bridge, wanting to test the shipmail again, or at least to look at the ocean from a good vantage.

Hannah picked up, excited. 'Yes, come up — you need to see this.' When I opened the bridge door, she was already pointing. 'We think it's still the Atlantic. It must be. Storm on the horizon.' The horizon looked the same to me — maybe a little dirtier. A smudge of clouds. Hannah was nodding at it, willing it to come. Visibility was about four miles. After that the ocean faded out. Hannah directed the ship towards it. At first, the only change to the mellow waters was a ripple effect across the surface of what had been dead calm for days. Then a churning started under the ship — boiling, as though the ocean were reacting to some enormous heat source, except that the temperature plummeted. Small showers passed over us. Waves built, spraying foam up the sides.

'That's the way,' said Hannah.

When the swell came, it was from the north-west, and we were pitching into it. But when we changed course, we were rolling. My mind flashed to my cabin: my laptop only half on the sticky mats, papers strewn, keys and medicine and chairs and a bin full of pads and tissues — all these flying on a roll. The rain pinged at the metal of the deck like bullets. Giant windscreen wipers, like that of a truck. I held onto the map table, then a chair — feet apart and planted. While the whole ship tilted, bucked, I staggered my way out onto the deck to let the rain belt at me. My back to the windows, front to the sea, arms splayed. The rain came stronger and harder, stinging me with the reality of the rising waves, the lack of land — either before or below us — my whole life missing. Alek stuck her head out. The captain had commanded me back. Inside, Hannah pointed at me. 'Don't get all existential.' I sluiced the water off my face and she calmed. 'You've still got pregnancy hormones going through you. It lasts a while.'

'Have you had an abortion?' I asked. The ship tilted wildly. It was both the worst and the best time for this question. Hannah set the ship to pitching directly into the rain — more stable. Eventually, she turned her attention back to me.

'People always ask that.'

'Have you?'

'No,' she said. 'The reason I refuse to answer — to media anyway — is because it's irrelevant. You don't fight for something ...' She pulled the control right back, so we were barely firing — using the power of the swell to propel us forwards in rhythmic bursts. 'You don't fight for something just because it's personal.' The ship gave a heave and settled. I realised I was clutching my chair, that my stomach was still sore, and my heart — well. 'I have a seven-year-old at home,' Hannah went on. 'With my husband.' I found it hard to hide my surprise.

'Does your kid know what you do?'

The rain intensified. Hannah yelled her response. 'Sure. Of course. He doesn't know what it means, though.' She grinned and turned back to the streaming windows. 'He's mostly excited that I work on a ship.'

The storm grew thicker, lashing the decks. The huge drops of rain burst at every window and porthole. In the chaos, Hannah grew calm, her movements slow, meditative. The rain was so thick we wouldn't have been able to see land if it were right in front of us. The sound, so soothing in other contexts, was white noise at full volume. I retreated, buried myself in the cabin pillows until I heard voices and footsteps, people running down the hall. Clutching my way back up to the bridge in the stomach of the storm. The waves like walls before us. We pitched so steeply that I fell, convinced we'd clear the crest and tip nose first into the depths. On my hands and knees in the control room, I recalled my parents' bedroom where I once found my mother kneeling. I thought she was praying but her face, when she raised it, was striped red with tears, a look in her eyes that said she'd never heard of God. I just have a tummy ache, she said and beckoned me closer, but I had backed away. I'd heard at school about 'women's troubles', but there was something about her body that I didn't want to touch. Something uneasy, separate to motherhood or marriage. I left her alone and went to seek out my dad and sister, telling them nothing.

The crew, when I found them on the lower levels, were surging around the fishtailing ship, slamming into walls and clinging to doors like life rafts. They screamed their words, emphatically, desperately. In the kitchen, where water poured in through the extractor fan, Mina told me how, in a typhoon on their last trip to Ireland, she found a sense of peace she'd never known, but now this storm had taken it away from her. In the slippery, tilting stairwell, Fa'iqah said she just wanted to be home with her boys — a partner, two sons, even the dog. Down in the dripping engine room, Marg said that she couldn't stand to be on land anymore with her wife — the ocean was the only place she felt alive. She wanted them to be together on the ship, but her wife had kids, couldn't do it. We were yelling over the sound of the engine that Marg was playing like an instrument. I wondered if we might be nearing land after all, given the magnitude of the storm.

'Go look,' Marg hollered back. I used the guardrail to get back up to the bridge and waited until the pitch was in my favour before I leaned on the door to get in. Hannah and Fa'iqah were there, frantic at the Morse code; calling

'Mayday, mayday' into the dead system.

'Can you see it?' I screamed. They shook their heads, staring into a tempest so dense it formed a mass. I thought: *I've come so far from home to get access to my body.* I thought: *if this is America, there is no America. Has there ever been?*

PORTHOLE

The wind over the highway bridge knocked them sideways through the autumn. They'd learned to take the short way through the fields but Tane always lingered, pointing at cows.

'Every stage of their miserable lives.'

It drove Steve fucking crazy, but he waited on the path, calling, 'Come on, son, this is your future', like Tane was twelve instead of just eighteen.

When Tane leaves — that first winter anyway — Steve doesn't know what to do except to keep up his walk across the field path alone. If he heads off at dawn, the mist on the mountains is another breath beside him. Fog making ghosts of fences. Paddocks stretched to white. Young cow's backs billowing steam. He focuses on the animal's breathing and on the path he's cutting — different from the one he's worn from house to the closest supermarket in town. It had caught him by surprise when Tane's mum drove off in the car and never returned, as though the world had sucked the breath out of him. Gasping in his new life, Steve had focused on the things he could reach: Tane, his home, checkout number two at PAK'nSAVE.

'Bobby, bobby, bobby,' Steve whispers now, because that's what Tane called them. 'Bobby.' On the other side of the fields, the industry-connection tutor, Melissa, is waiting in learning block A to bridge those missed years of high school by teaching Steve not to call them bobbies. Their massive eyes and enquiring tongues, Steve's fingers through the wire. Often when he reaches the underpass below the paddock road, the grown-up cows are already tromping purposefully over it and, beyond them, the industrial funnels at the top of the prac buildings are blasting their mystery steams. Now the pass is empty, the fields around it abandoned.

'I will if you will, Dad,' Tane said when Steve found the course online. It meant making a new route to include the technical college. Tane worked with Steve on it. From the house to the corner by the toilet block and car park. Then, a turn away from the familiar path into town to the shops. Steve looked for his wife's face in each passing car as they crossed the highway to the start of the bridge — ducked his head into his elbow to pretend his panicked panting was a coughing fit. He felt Tane's light fingers on his shoulder and clutched his phone to his heart, the well-meaning woman's voice mispronouncing the streets. They arrived on the first day furrowed, stress sweating through their hoodies. Tane was so relieved, he blithely went around introducing his dad to all the strangers and Steve let him, did his best not to have another attack in front of the boy's new friends. Now he repeats 'Bovine Respiratory Disease Complex' in the dim tunnel. He can't face 'Pasteurella Haemolytica'. Sounds too much like a woman's name. Makes him blush angrily in the dark. Even knowing that Melissa arrives for their Tuesday morning class in a steely blue car (he once saw her lock it, then go back for a Tupperware) is overwhelming.

He picks up his pace, stumbling, catching himself on the sharp stones. Around the corner the cows are gathered in one of the holding yards, a tight mass of heat and mud. Instinctively he reaches for Tane — who has long disembarked at a southern bus station and to whom a message now seems impossible. A cow glances at the space where Tane should be and curls an impossible tongue. 'Hey there. Hey,' Steve says. But what to say to a son? Tane so far beyond home, shops, tutorial, that Steve can't picture it without feeling throat punched.

'Hi,' says Melissa from behind the animal. She removes a long latex glove. Her eyes are red. Steve nods at the door to building A, beyond which is a coffee machine. 'How about Tane?' asks Melissa.

'I was only doing this to get him through.'

'You should keep on, Stephen. We're up to cannulation.'

'Cannulation,' Steve tries, but it doesn't come out right. Melissa moves away to shift some lengths of plastic piping around and Steve is lost in it.

The hot coffee is bitter on the workshop table beside Tane's copy of *Livestock* — early feverish notes in the margins from before they ever saw the cows. Poetry, some of them. Beside 'cannulation, commonly called porthole surgery', Tane has written in red all caps, 'SEE YOUR FUTURE'. When Steve thinks of his future, he sees Tane: the thin freckly arms of long ago, as well as where he imagines him now — washing dishes in a nice cafe in Dunedin or serving out the front. A week or so back, not long after Tane moved out, Steve accepted a FaceTime with Joanne. She was distracted by something off-screen throughout their chat, asked if he was into tarot cards. When he told her he saw the future as being about young people, like Tane, she'd finally looked deep into the camera and asked to meet in person. He told her he had the flu. During their second FaceTime, she described her difficult labour, and he had to turn off his microphone for some deep breaths. Later she messaged that she couldn't be with someone who was scared of the female body. The door to the study room pushes open. Steve hides his face in the coffee rim.

'It's a demonstration today, Stephen. A prac,' says Melissa. 'Attendance is assessed.'

'I'm just waiting.'

Melissa glances out the window with a look so indistinguishable from hope that Steve wonders if she's waiting, too, only the past is sucking so strongly away from them they can't even fathom the future.

'The others have started gearing up,' she tells him and leaves.

Out in the yard the cows and the students stare at each other over rough, wet concrete. The cows are intimidatingly close, their bulk and their nakedness. Some of them have red targets on their sides. The students — mostly late teenagers like Tane — look coltish in their white coats and turn their fearful eyes on Melissa, like they fully expect her to appear with a gun. Even when she dons her gloves again with practiced calm, the class backs collectively into the bendy metal guardrail. Melissa reaches for the target on one of the cows and opens a little door in its side. She draws the students forwards. It's dark in there — a window to an inner world that the cow will never see.

'It allows access to the first area of the cow's stomach, and examination of the digestive system,' Melissa tells them. 'And today I'm going to show you how it's done. We do this to improve production, make smarter milk. This is advanced stuff, but I hope it will inspire you. You know, for further study.' Steve shuffles forwards a little to watch the technician lead in a new, whole cow — without a door — and to shave mesmeric circles into its side. He finds he's at the front and tries to stand tall, hand on one hip, to encourage the younger students. The technician washes the cow's shaved side again, starting in the middle and scrubbing in ever widening circles at the clipped fur — as though a picture is being revealed — while Melissa says things about sterilisation and antibiotics. The hand moves round and around. The cow stays still but for her soft brown ear, an antenna.

One of the students wants to ask a question. 'Is it like a massage?"

Melissa laughs. 'Sure, like that. We're making sure the site doesn't get contaminated.' Melissa withdraws long needles and plunges them one by one into the cow's side, explaining how procaine hydrochloride is injected for numbing. The animal bucks against the stall. Melissa frowns at the cow. 'I don't know why she's so unhappy today.'

They all get a break while the anaesthetic takes hold. Steve looks at his son's last message: 'i got a lift thnx x'. That day, Steve watched the microwave clock until the time he knew Tane's bus had left from the Square. Now he types 'did you get there safe love dad'. If Tane is looking at his message thread at exactly the same time he will see the little dots like tracks to show Steve is thinking about him and writing something. Steve deletes the message before it's sent and gets another coffee from the machine. Back in the yards, the prac cow stares ahead in the stall, ears still searching for signal. The students filter back and watch her shaved side like it's a screen and they're about to see a movie. Melissa has cold red cheeks and a scalpel. She smiles, turns, and cuts a perfect circle in the cow's side with the knife. The students fall silent, watching her remove the layer of fur with a tweezer, revealing meat. The cow's ear still moving, sound without feeling. Steve shuffles. Bumps into a student dressed all in black. He can't take his eyes off Melissa, who is making a vertical incision and sticking her entire fist in the hole. The cow panics. The technician moves to the front to check the restraints. Steve sinks further into the bodies.

Tane's voice through the small crowd. 'You okay?'

Steve turns, his vision blurred. His son's hand. He grabs, then loses it. The young woman holds her fingers like they're bitten.

'Sorry,' Steve says. 'Sorry.'

Melissa looks up from where she's pulling part of the cow's stomach out through the hole. '... the rumen. Everything alright back there?'

Steve keeps his face to the front and edges around the students by sound and feel. Steps on a foot, shuffles to the left. A surprised yelp, a little to the right. The cow backs away, too, but the tether stops her. She's pulled up, whereas Steve can move further and further away. Melissa draws a rubber ring from a bucket of hot water and holds it up with her gloved hand to demonstrate how soft and flexible it is. 'The cannula.' She pushes it against the hole in the cow, who writhes and kicks. Steve reaches the metal guard. He is stopped, too, and a low note comes out of him. The ghost that is his living son chuckles at the noise.

'You sound like that cow, Dad.'

The other students are staring, so he slides along the barrier until it gives way and he's free, clattering across the holding yards.

The sun is sharp through the cloud where Steve sits bent over his knees at the entrance to the college, but it's also raining — pinpricks on his back.

'Sunshower, Dad,' says Tane.

'I still don't get how.' It was one of the things they'd argued about when they walked over the fields. Tane didn't really know the answer either, but he didn't see a problem with sun and rain together. They always meant to look it up. Steve turns to see Melissa brisk-walking down the path towards him and hunches over again.

'How are you?' she asks, voice pointed as rain.

Steve waits a moment before answering. He wants it to come out human. 'I'm alright.'

'Coming back in?'

'I don't know, Mel.'

There's a silence in which the rain stops. 'This is a

compulsory attendance, Stephen.'

He sits up, but it doesn't feel good, so he leans over again. 'I could do a written assignment,' he tells his knees.

'You have to do this to pass.' The sound of metal falling on concrete back in the yards and an exclamation. 'Stephen?'

It's easier for Steve to just stare at the moss taking eternity to break apart the concrete with its green fingers.

'This is your assessment. They're livestock ...' Melissa leans in, hisses, 'they're *cows*.'

Then he's upright, looking at Melissa, who is red. She says something about checking whether he can do a written after all, given his difficulties. Her quick footsteps back to the yard, clapping her hands to bring all the students together.

'"Mel", huh?' Tane says somewhere beside him, laughter like sunlight.

It's really starting to come down. The perpetually wet yards are drier than outside now. The students have bunched around the warm cow, partly out of necessity — the rain's sideways drizzling — and partly to hear Melissa, who shouts her lesson. A neat cap like a door has been placed over the cannula. It's a joke cow now, rather than the victim of some gruesome invasion.

'What do you call a cow with a door in its side?' Steve whispers to Tane. The student turns to him.

'What?'

'Sorry.'

'But what's the punchline?'

'A porthole,' Melissa tells the group. The low winter sun fights its way back through the cloud bank and slides on an angle into the yards. Melissa walks through the cluster of students with her arms outstretched — the rain-sparkled sun making a halo of the frizz of her hair — herding them so they can look at the cannula up close. She glances at Steve and away again but there's no heat to her expression. 'Just open it up like a porthole,' she tells him and every student. The cow stands there peaceably enough.

'Probably doped,' says Tane.

'What would you know about that?' Steve whispers but smiles, ribbing him. The student in line behind him smiles back.

'Your turn, old mate,' she says.

The cow is enormous before him. Steaming in the sunlight. The porthole leaking some of her secrets down her side. Steve takes a breath and fiddles with the little rubber lever.

'This is exciting,' he tells the cow. There is a sucking — the cow's skin shivers — and the door gives way to a dark interior.

'Do you see it?' Tane whispers. 'Do you see your future?'

Steve looks and looks and looks into the meaty darkness.

GETAWAYS

Julie didn't have an online presence or anything. It was hard to work out whether she was missing or dead. The police caught up with her at Tin Can Bay.

'Aren't I allowed to go somewhere?' Julie asked.

'Well, you can do whatever you want, but your kids are worried because we found your car. And there's the use of resources in locating you. We'll let them know but you should really make contact. Unless there's something —'

'They're just *so rude*.' Julie got tears in her eyes remembering Christmas day. 'I can't stand it.'

It was really awkward for the police to have to tell the children she wasn't coming back — Anjelica the daughter and Josh the son, Caucasian, mid- to late-thirties, own children running about. So, when Julie called twelve years later, Josh wasn't particularly receptive. Mostly, he didn't want to deal with his sister.

'Ghost us and your grandkids and then come back when you're out of cash?'

'I need somewhere to live, Josh. It's impossible at this age.

And my hip.'

'No way.' But he did tell Anjelica, who insisted that Julie
go and live with Josh. He and his wife had the bigger house
and they'd put in a pool. Everyone came over for welcome
home takeaway and stared at Julie over the dining table. Josh
said something about the cost of living, and Anjelica pushed
past Julie to get at the garlic bread. Actually, so did Josh's son,
who still lived at home.

My *god*, thought Julie.

RANGING

Then, when they're down to the dregs of their tea and huddled bright under the spotlight on the landing above the concrete stairs, someone says: *I dare you*.

'I dare you to go out there. Run down the street or whatever.'

Strange to be so near the highway — the turn-off just a few streets away — and so dark and quiet, an ocean emptied. Lauren mutters that *she'll* do it, and Felicity glances up from where she's locking the hall. Lauren hardly makes a sound in group. Her sister drops her off right at the steps and she walks up them in boots with a heel, her jaw yellowing now after all those purple weeks. But there's a voice in Lauren. She'll run down the empty, broken street, she tells them, until they can't see her.

'Then, I'll whoop.'

'Whoop?'

'Yeah, like —' she whoops.

'Quiet,' Cammy hisses.

No one comes, not their partners or the security guards. Not their sons who have up and left, never seen since. Felicity looks down the street anyway for Kaleb's stout legs, small replicas of hers and nothing like his bandy father. She stays so still — they all stay so still in the collective vision of Felicity's three-and-a-half-year-old, who never appears, of course — that the sensor light shuts off over them.

Only two months back, under that same light, an elderly man from the Royal Serviceman's League told Felicity she couldn't use the hall for group. It would attract the wrong sort, he said.

'We're survivors of the wrong sort, not the inflictors,' Felicity told him, then returned with her brother who shrugged and said, sure, he'd sit outside — security or reassurance or whatever. So the old man had handed over the key.

'You need these meetings, too,' Felicity said to Donald in the car on the way home. 'I really started them for you.' She touched her brother's hand; he flinched. Now the old man, her brother, her brother's husband, her son, she supposes her ex, too — deleted his number — gone. Those who remain arrive at the hall each week like they're summoned. They arrive with lollies and peanuts and whatever they can find on the dwindling shelves; Cammy brings a kettle because the front door key doesn't open the other rooms of the hall. Out of the bedroom and into the night, Felicity thinks, if they want to. She spends her evenings at the lounge-room window scrolling news sites, looking for Kaleb.

·

Felicity drags her seat into the circle of others and tries to
get Lauren talking. Gives up and turns to the only other one
who looks ready to engage tonight.

'You haven't shared for a few weeks, Barb.'

Barb sighs and points out that even though one source
of violence has disappeared, it doesn't mean it's all over. 'The
men have gone but it never stops for me, does it?'

The white women in the room shift uncomfortably in
their plastic chairs. Now it's Felicity who can't meet the eye
of the Gunaikurnai woman. She finds an encouraging smile.

'Let's talk about that.'

Barb laughs. 'I don't think so. We'll sort it out ourselves.
I'm just saying.'

'Perhaps. Perhaps you have a memory you'd like to share
instead?'

Barb nods slowly. 'I've got a memory but it's also an
analogy.' She leans forwards. 'Don't you think all of this is
like being at after school sports?' A few in the group look up.
'You know: it's cold, you have to go around the field doing
all different things, high jump, long jump, sprints. You're
way over on one side of the oval, and the boys are playing
in the distance, but you're there with your girlfriends,
and they've already done their events, and they're waiting
to cheer you on.' The group is quiet, lost in memories of
running at night.

Felicity says, 'That's such a good way to frame it, Barb.
We're here together, and we have to be distanced from them,
but they're still part of our lives, our memories. Do other
people want to comment?'

'But then,' Barb continues, 'one of your friends says,
"You'll win, Barb, because you're a Tyler." And you're apart

again. Not one of your group and not over with your
brothers either. Alone.'

Felicity swallows audibly. A chair creaks. Barb sits back.
'Who else?' No one speaks. 'Come on. I shared.'

'This isn't the same,' Sal says finally. 'But it's reminded me
how when I get home my twins will be fighting, guaranteed.'

'How old are they?'

'Almost thirteen,' Sal says. 'They never fought when
Kenneth was around. They loved him. He taught them
Japanese from his homework. When he was home, they
whispered and giggled. How much space did my son take
up? Now I walk out, and I can hear them yelling from the
carport, and I keep going because I know as long as they
don't kill each other they'll be fine.'

Barb nods at this to hide a shaky breath. If she thinks
about her brothers beyond the oval, even just Luke's voice,
she'll lose it in this circle. She glances up to see who's noticed
— group can be a spotlight — but everyone is looking at
Cammy because she's spitting with sobs.

'But where's my boyfriend?' Tears pool under Cammy's
eyes. 'I mean where the hell have they gone?'

When the hour is up, they clump on the outside landing. Sal
kicks her sneaker out over the top of the outside stairs —
she's going down, back to her car.

'Nudie run, Sally?' someone yells.

Felicity flinches — so odd to hear that high voice call out
loudly, explicitly, but also how wonderful. Sal is standing on
the step facing them as though on a sunken stage, miming
lifting her top, and they're hooting like those they've lost.

The catcalls and urges to take it all off melting into the night. Then Sal walks down the remaining stairs and just does it. Rips off her blue T-shirt and dumps it on the ground. Stands there in an old grey bra slightly too small and eyes Lauren. The other woman smiles, glances back at the group who've fallen silent, and slowly lifts her top, too. She's got on one of those comfortable sports bras. No hoots from the group now, just encouragement.

'Go on, girls. You can do it.' Like teenagers at sports. Like women taking their bras off so matter-of-factly, Sal with her hooks and Lauren stretching the material, to drop them next to the T-shirt on the concrete. Sal says that one of the last things her son said to her was about his dirty clothes on the bathroom floor. Felicity can't remember the last thing her son said. She was asleep. He was asleep, too, beside her, after not sleeping much of the night before. She only remembers his absence from the bed, the cold grass on the nature strip, screaming his name to find other mothers and sisters outside screaming, too.

'Is he really gone?' Lauren asks. She means all of them.

Sal nods. 'Gone.'

Then they turn and they're gone, too. Streaking down the suburban street, their cries and whoops rhythmic. One by one the others follow, in their bras or not. Jogging steadily over the car park and away. Barb is left with fiddly buttons on a shirt. She starts to rip at them, panicked, there half-naked at the hall. Listens for the grumble of a car, footsteps in the leaf litter, boots on the stairs. Turns, breath caught, to see Felicity on the landing.

Breathes out. 'Coming?'

Felicity shakes her head. 'I need to ...' she jangles the keys to the hall. 'These have to be returned.'

'Tonight?' There's no one to return them to.

'Anyway,' Felicity says, thinking of her brother. 'This group is for you.'

Barb finally gets the last button and stands there in a seriously lacy number, properly fitted. Felicity wonders if it was bought before the husband disappeared, or after. Barb sticks out a hand, show-tune style.

'It's not about the tits,' she says.

'What's it about then?' Felicity whispers.

'Being able to just ...' Barb grabs Felicity's hand, keys and all, and they launch off the bottom step into the darkness.

THIS TIME

The extinction came I felt it was me   killed everything
I knew   (did nothing to stop it) because polar bears
filled my feed   I was starting to look at Hope differently
—   the quiet student wrote a poem for my class   really
promising I wrote 'promising' on the world   I stopped
sleeping in the summer we went to the reef   the bright fish
bleached empty

A SENSATION OF WHIRLING
AND A LOSS OF BALANCE

It was all very fine. Nothing really happened. There were layers of supreme matt around Tanya's eyes, and when I called her 'Tanya' instead of 'Mum' she looked relieved. That's the thing: when you've been away you can't tell whose history you're in when you get back. Is it yours? Is it theirs? Is it in a photograph you stared at on the shared computer until the person who had been waiting had waited long-a-fucking-'nough? I watched Tanya's mouth move. When she pursed her lips, the hairs on her face that were white with foundation bowed into the cracks.

On the plastic lace tablecloth there were cupcakes and dips, a bread hollowed out with cheese put inside and baked or something. There were no drinks except for cordial. Everyone had their own plastic cup, and you could write your name on yours with a permanent marker. Gary was there with a cup labelled 'Gary'. I would have said I was surprised that he and Tanya were still talking except they weren't, really. His cordial had an amber tinge, and when I followed Tanya from one room to the next, I caught a whiff of him: whiskey-warm and perilous. My cousins were there, too, smiling and stooping as though the crosses around their necks both weighed and supported them. They'd visited me while I was away, at least twice, so I didn't feel the need to stop. I trailed Tanya right across the lounge room rug until it turned back to regular carpet and then became bathroom. Tanya disappeared behind the door.

I was in the lounge room with the rest of the guests: those cousins still smiling, another Christian couple, some more people who looked as familiar as extras on a TV show. I needed some of that cordial that Gary was drinking by the kitchen door, because I'd just noticed my sister was there, too, in a frame beside the television. Tanya hadn't thought to pull her down (or she *had* thought, too much. She'd probably been propping that frame up and down all morning until those Christians had told her that memories are close to Godliness). I met a lot of Christians while I was away and I get where they're coming from, I do, but who can remember all the rules? Love someone and not someone else. Don't fork food off someone else's plate. Eat fish. Something something neighbour.

Loral was in the lounge room, too, still with that avalanche of a face. Tanya would have told her that she's my best friend so she had to be there (Tanya told me the same thing), but Loral wouldn't look at me. She kept her droopy eye fixed on the cheese ball and crackers. Other than that, there was just a few busy kids trying to coax something out from under the couch. Those kids had been dressed up in some sort of extreme party wear I didn't even *know* came in kids' sizes. They were like awful dolls, quietly convincing the darkness under the couch to come out into the light. At first, I pinned those kids on the Christians-that-weren't-my-cousins, but then another kid in an amazing mustard skivvy slid up to them and the Christian dad put his arm across the boy's chest like a seatbelt and he was safe. The other doll kids, loose in the world as spare change, must have belonged to the TV extras.

What I needed was Gary. I blinked desperately at the space he and his drink had left and then I smelled his cigarette smoke feeling its way through the open back door and into the lounge. I wanted one of them, too, so I followed the smoke, but Gary wasn't on the porch. He was at the far end of the yard, messing with something by the fence. A hole. I couldn't tell if he was trying to make it bigger or smaller. I would have gone out there and bugged him about it, but Tanya came out of the bathroom behind me and fluffed her hair and smiled. There were more layers, dark and wet as concrete, over the old ones on her face. I stuck my gaze on her like my eyeballs were arms wrapped around her leg, and she was nineteen and I was only three and dressed in corduroy pants and a T-shirt I had picked myself. One with a dolphin that had been printed so the snout went under my armpit, and I could trap it there. Without a snout, a dolphin looks like a pumped-up blue tyre. I don't know what my sister would have worn. In the picture beside the TV, she wasn't wearing anything. She was just a head. When I tried to imagine her body below that I got dizzy and had to sit on the couch for a while.

Tanya hadn't planned for dinner, but Gary stayed stuck to the door like sugar, sucking on that Gary cup. I thought that making something that we could all eat standing up would be easiest, but Tanya said, 'Now that everyone's left you start talking? That's good, that's really great.' And I realised I should help more. I spilled cordial on the plastic lace tablecloth, and Tanya seemed like she would have a nervous breakdown so Gary unstuck himself and took the jug away from me. I got pretty strong while I was away, but I also got better at people. I understood that Gary and my mother were at least fucking, and maybe even thinking about something serious again, so I let go my hold of the jug and tried to look Gary in the eye. I only got as far as his clean-shaven chin before I had to wipe my cordially hand on my jeans. The TV extras had gone, and so had Loral and my cousins, but the Christians were still in the kitchen with their skivvy kid, and in the lounge room the two doll children were pressed against the carpet with their faces under the couch.

'Who do you belong to?' I asked them. There was something going on in the next room between Gary, Tanya, and the plastic lace that I didn't want to be a part of. The kids seemed the safer option.

'He just lives here,' one of the kids said. They both had their faces under the couch, and they were little — eight or nine years old — so I wasn't sure which of them spoke: the boy (who for all I could tell was wearing lederhosen), or the girl that someone had dressed as a human meringue. When I didn't answer, the girl pulled her face into the light, and that face was a red, round, miniature version of the Christian dad in the kitchen.

'Is he yours?' she asked me.

I glanced at the boy. 'Isn't he *your* brother?'

'Yes, but the little dog.'

I got down on my knees, which was hard on them, and that's a sad thing for a twenty-three-year-old to say. The space under the couch was empty of everything — dust, coins, blankets, shoes — except a creature about the size of two fists. Its eyes shone out from way down against the wall. I smiled at it. I thought my teeth might make a light in the dark. It didn't growl; it didn't do anything.

'Why are you dressed like a boy?'

I ducked my head out. It was the girl. 'You can talk,' I said. She looked down at her froth in confusion. 'That's just the way we talk where I've been. We talk rough to each other and that way we're friends. We also test each other. Like, I bet you could get that dog out if you —'

'We're getting takeaway,' said Tanya behind us. I *was* on the ground with those two children, but I didn't think she should look at me the way she did, with all the makeup slid forwards on her face and her eyes shining like the dog's.

'Is that your dog?' I asked her. I was living here now so I thought I should know.

'You want Chinese? Or there's pizza but it's not good.'

I wanted Tanya to recall that I used to live here before with her and my sister, so I knew about the takeaway options, but I was on the floor with these children. Somewhere under the couch, the creature was looking at how my jeans had ridden down to show a smiling, toothless crack.

We got pizza. Tanya had the table all set up, but when it came, we took the plastic plates and cups and sat in front of the TV and watched *The Simpsons* in silence until the news came on, and everyone relaxed a bit in front of a civil war and some robbery that went so badly you could laugh. I laughed. Tanya and the Christians — the mum, the dad, the three kids — stared at me. Even Gary stared. I glanced under the couch expecting to see the two button eyes of the little dog staring, too, but it kept itself to itself.

The Christians thought it was time to take their kids home. The doll children ran out to their station wagon without a backwards glance, but the skivvy kid said such a formal goodbye to me and Tanya and Gary that I was moved to shake his hand. He had a strong, bony grip. I realised he was probably thirteen and could almost date my sister in the picture because she was not quite fifteen there. I wanted to give him some sage advice — 'Don't go away, kiddo', or better, 'Don't get done' — but the Christian dad was honking the car with un-Christian impatience. I was left alone in the doorway of the house. When the car had gone, I realised I could just walk out into the cool night. Unless I left the state, no one cared. When you stand on a cliff's edge it's not vertigo that makes you fall, it's your body just naturally wanting to fling itself off whatever high thing it can. And you have to put a stop to it.

I shut the door and went back inside. There were noises coming from Tanya's room. With my ear pressed against the cold paint I could hear them. Not sex noises, but more talking than either had done at the party. Gary rumbled and Tanya laughed, and then it seemed like she was crying. They'd turned off the heating, but they hadn't put away the cordial or Gary's jacket. In the inner pocket was a hip flask of whiskey, three quarters drunk, a half soft-pack of cigarettes, some notes and coins, a winning lottery scratch-it for fifteen dollars, and a pill without a blister. I popped the pill then upended the whiskey into a nameless plastic cup, filled the rest with the cordial, and made myself comfortable on the couch. My old room was filled with sewing stuff and boxes, and it didn't have a bed. I could sleep on that couch.

I guess it had been five years and four-and-a-half months since I'd drunk anything that wasn't home brewed in a plastic bag. Soon enough my head came unstuck and floated up around the light fixture. From there I could see tomorrow. Gary and I would clean out my room and fix a bed and maybe a desk and a lamp in there, some drawers to put my underpants and jeans. My head bumped against the lightbulb, and I could see into the past. I showed my sister how to go into other people's houses but not how to leave. I smacked my forehead on the roof and could see the present. The little woolly dog crept from under the couch and stared at me like my sister in the picture on the mantel stared at me. My head floated down and made a soft landing on my neck. The dog's eyes and my sister's eyes were much the same. They were both very round and very small, and they shone with their own brown light. I didn't know the dog's name, so I called it Comet. My sister liked flying and heaven and things.

I took my plastic cup into the kitchen and rattled around until I found an open sherry next to the soy sauce and cooking oil. Comet and my sister were still in the lounge room, staring. I took a sip of the sherry and stared back. My head loosened again but stayed attached to my neck.

'Comet,' I said. The dog didn't respond so I tried calling my sister, 'Amy.' My voice snagged on the 'y' and the dog stood up. I said it again. 'Amy. Come on Amy.' The dog tottered out behind me.

The backyard was cold and bright with stars and a wonky moon. I lit one of Gary's cigarettes and sucked so deep my throat caught on fire. I didn't choke though. I always told my sister, *you've got to be quiet*, but she never got it. When the smoke came out, we were near the hole that Gary had been bothering at the fence. It was about the size of the little dog. A pile of dirt lay at its edge. I tapped the dirt with my sneaker and some of it crumbled and disappeared. The dog made to follow it.

'Wait up, Amy.' I put my smoke in my mouth and got down on my hands and knees and peered in. It wasn't a hole; it was a tunnel. The moon shone through on the other side where I knew there was a paddock thick with rabbits and crickets and cheat grass and not much else. When I sat back the dog was staring intently, its black nose snuffling through to all those things on the other side. 'Go on then.' I pointed at the tunnel. That dog might have been small, but it had sense enough to not come out from under a couch when there were kids around, and sense enough to get into a hole when there was fun on the other side. Only after its tail had disappeared did I think about how it might not have the sense to come back.

TERRITORY

They meet in a gash of clear fell where you can see the sky. Marko turns his car engine off and the woman beside him strokes her long, black-painted nails like they're pets. Outside, Scotty has the buggy unloaded and gives it a few revs. His dog is still in the cage, quiet at the sound. Scotty revs again. He has a new baby and Marko knows full well: he needs the noise. After a while Marko leans out the window into the heat.

We going or what?

Scotty leaves the buggy by some stumpy trees, half dead already from burn-off, and hands Marko a can of beer.

They'll know we're here if you keep revving it, Marko tells him.

Scotty smiles around the can.

We'll fucken find them.

Scotty laughs with apple cheeks that look stuffed like a glazed pig. The sun is all over them now, low.

Boars before whores, Scotty mutters.

Marko laughs silently out the window so the woman

can't see him. He finishes his can, mashes it slowly against the side of the car, and throws it into the bush.

This is Sarah, says Marko.

Sarah? Scotty sounds surprised.

Yeah. She's got a kid.

Sarah gets out of the car and comes around to shake Scotty's hand. Marko can see Scotty really trying not to look at her legs out of the jean shorts.

I've got a beautiful five-year-old called Amelia. Started school this year.

Scotty's face becomes even more surprised.

You must've had her young.

Marko laughs and spit comes out. He opens the car door to stand by Sarah.

Don't worry about Scotty, he's shit-faced already.

I bet he just says what everyone's thinking.

Sarah's hair is blonde like all of them, but she's got fox teeth and a dark mole like a beauty spot slipped down from her lip to her chin. She's wearing a pink polo shirt. Scotty plunges his hand in the ice to get more beers. He hands one to Sarah.

Here you go. Put hair on your chest.

Sarah opens the ring, and says, Best part of the day.

Where'd you two meet again?

Scotty just wants the story.

He just wants the story, Marko tells Sarah.

It's a good story, says Sarah.

She takes another swig of the beer. Scotty's given her low alcohol, but she could probably handle full strength. *Love my baby, my beers, and my boars*, she wrote on the page, and there was a photo of her looking the same as she does now

— no surprises there. She got fifty-four likes before Marko even saw it, and over 100 in the days after. He waited to comment, let all the other guys write *hi sweetie* and *youll love me to* — then he wrote *want to come with me for a creek run on Sunday?* Straight up.

Marko's two dogs are in a cage up the back of his pickup — a bitch called Dingo and a big mutt called Rabies. Rabies is just there to scare the shit out of them, but Dingo is the real deal. Scotty brought along his house dog with its messed-up muzzle. When he opens the cage, his dog looks like it'd rather stay there. Sarah is looking at Marko's dogs, especially Dingo, who's fluffy around the scars.

You got a dog?

Nah. My ex did. Stupid dog went for a swim and we never saw him again. My ex said maybe he's just living on a community or something.

Marko shakes his head, Croc meat.

Sarah nods. Stupid dog.

Marko went swimming in the East Alligator River, Scotty pipes up.

Marko drains his beer and pegs the can at Scotty's guts. But Sarah's looking. Marko takes a breath and the air is hot. It's too late for a run. Scotty will just fuck around with his buggy all day if he gets half the chance.

We were road running, says Marko.

He gets the metal chest plate out and straps it to Dingo, who gets a different look in her dog eyes: chest plate means working.

Anyway, Dingo here got in the water, and I called her,

but she was swimming over to the other side — same as your dog probably — so I just jumped in and got her.

Sarah glances at Scotty and they laugh.

In the East Alligator?

Marko swam halfway across the thing — what's that, forty metres? — crocs fucken everywhere, so black you couldn't even see, and then he swam all the way back with the dog.

Scotty's lips are wet with beer.

Had to get lifted out because the sides are too slippery and so there he was waiting in the water, in the dark, with his dog and the crocs.

She's a fucking good dog, says Marko. I wasn't willing to let go of her. A tough, mean, fighting machine dog that don't take shit from nothing.

They all look at Dingo, who looks back at them with dark, working-dog eyes.

Just like you, aye Marko? Scotty says.

Sarah gets into the buggy next to Scotty and Marko stands on the tray with the dogs. Sarah is mashed up against the gear stick, and Marko can see Scotty's hand through the window, pressing on Sarah's thigh every time he has to change gear. The road is blocked by a log, so Scotty turns off the track and knocks over three stubby trees. They get stuck on one and Scotty revs the engine until that's all there is. They'll be heard in the hollows and all along the creek. Scotty drives the buggy up over it and the dead trunk cracks like bones. They lurch back onto the dirt road. The dogs grip the metal tray.

Go right here, Scotty!

They fork off the track and into the bush. Scotty smashes a few more trees. Marko raps on the roof and they stop.

I'll drive you up to the creek, Scotty shouts over the engine, but Marko jumps down and Dingo follows him. Marko has to order Rabies down. Scotty's dog peers at Marko over his busted muzzle but doesn't leave the tray.

With the engine off, it's just the sound of their boots cracking the ground. Marko hears Scotty pull the ring on another can back in the buggy.

You don't have to worry, Sarah says to Marko. I used to go out with my ex all the time. I won't talk once we're out there.

Marko stops and smiles at her.

It's pretty ace that you know the drill.

He glances at the strap around her shorts.

Even got your own knife.

Sarah touches the fake leather sheath.

It's his spare one — I've never used it, but.

Might get lucky today, Marko tells her then blushes.

He turns and starts walking through the bush. He can hear Sarah's footsteps behind. The ground glints with dead leaves, but the dirt underneath has been gnawed by the dry. They turn off, and head down the slope, and it gets cooler and cooler until they're at the creek bed. In a few months, where they're standing will be underwater, churning with crocodiles. Marko watches Dingo put her face to the dark shallows and test them with a few licks. Sometimes a croc wanders too far from the estuaries and gets stranded and hungry in the seasonal creeks. Marko glances at Sarah — she's watching the dog — but then Dingo takes off downstream. Marko follows. He can hear Sarah. Her footfalls are heavy but she's still better than Scotty. They come to where there's more mud than water, and Marko points to it. It has been trampled with hooves and wallowed in, cool and wet under the pandanus trees. They probably took off when Scotty started revving, almost an hour ago. He can't even smell them, but Dingo has something. Or had it. The dog looks desperately up at Marko then away again.

Good girl, Marko mutters and Dingo tries again. She sniffs along the creek away from the hollows, to where the water pools green, then black. It's so still there's a skin of dust over it. Dingo stops again and so does Marko, and after a moment Sarah's footsteps go quiet behind. They can still hear Rabies tromping around on the bank above, but Dingo is stock solid beside one of the pools. The quiet water swells. Marko hears Sarah take a breath. He puts a hand on his knife. An insect skids over the surface, breaking through the dust to stick to the water underneath.

The dog takes off again, up the bank. Marko can hear Sarah scrambling and slipping, but he leaves her to follow Dingo because the dog has started skipping on scent. She dances over it for a while, then changes direction and bolts off through the narrow paperbark trees ahead of Marko for 100 then 200 metres. Dingo reaches a high bank that buckles over the creek bed and then she's gone. It takes Marko only seconds to reach the bank, but Dingo is already barking, sharp as birdsong. Marko clears the edge and drops down to the dry creek bed where the dog's snarls ring out from a clay cave, and Marko can see the hind of a boar, its tail curled up and away from its heavy black balls. The boar disappears into the gloom but Dingo barks it out. In the brilliant light, the pig turns. Marko can see big white tusks at its jaw before the pig twists its body back to fight, but the chance is gone. Dingo makes the hit up — a high yelp that bounces around the river bed — and locks on to the pig's thick ear.

Rabies appears on the ridge and makes his way down to help keep the pig in place with deep belly barks. Marko wraps his hands around the boar's bony hind legs and grunts to lift him up. The pig has no neck — none of them do. It can't turn or move. Dingo is locked on, her body tucked in close behind the boar's ear so she can't get bitten. Marko strains to see again and catches the flash of bone from the lower jaw — teeth that hook in unbroken white arcs up past its snout and towards its little eye. The pig can't even close its mouth. He shouts up the bank.

Does it have fucken massive hooks or what?

Sarah is staring down at them.

Big. Real big.

Marko shifts his grip to hold tighter. Rabies barks and snaps at the boar.

Come on then, Marko calls up to Sarah.

She scans the bank, jumps and lands heavily but stands easily enough. Marko flips the boar to expose its chest. The pig is still now and hopeless. Sarah looks at Marko.

My ex always did this bit.

Marko moves his weight against the boar's.

Time to get the fuck over him?

Sarah scowls but steps in. Her knife's sharper than his and it goes right through the neck, but the pig is still breathing. Again, says Marko. She plunges it past the layer of black hair and pink skin so it's held in place by the flesh. Marko puts his hand over hers and jiggles until it starts gurgling with thick, dark blood. The pig feels it then. Takes a final breath and dies quiet.

How'd Sarah like it? Scotty asks when Marko runs back to the buggy.

Yeah, good.

Marko puts his hands on his knees and looks back through the bush to where Sarah would be if all the trees were gone. Scotty gets out of the buggy and points his hips at the side of the road. His piss sends up a low cloud of dust.

She's a nice girl, Scotty says over his shoulder. I'd fuck her.

He does a little jump to shake, and tucks himself in.

Would you fuck her?

Marko shrugs.

She's still hung up on her ex.

But if she can stick a pig …

Marko nods.

You should see the fucken great hooks on him.

Scotty fist punches the air and climbs in the buggy. They drive over the rough ground until Scotty gets stuck between a rock and a tree. He revs the buggy like a thing dying. Marko climbs out and runs. The sweat that dried starts up again and his legs take up their familiar burn. He runs until he reaches the bend at the end of the hollow where Sarah is crouched down in front of the boar. She has one hand to her ear and the other touching the dried black hair on the pig's bloodied snout. She looks like she's having words.

You right?

Sarah jolts and moves her phone from her ear to her pocket. She lifts her eyebrows. Still looks the same as in the profile picture. The angle of her head even.

Marko grins. Thought you were talking to the pig.

Sarah opens her mouth to answer, but the sound of the buggy burning through the bush eats up her words, and then Scotty appears, swerving and bucking. He hardly stops the buggy before he gets out and lurches down the bank towards the boar.

Fucken rippin'!

He gets down to pull out the stick that Marko shoved in its mouth. The jaw slips half closed against the tusks and then stops frozen, mid-bite forever. Scotty grips the sticky head and plants a kiss on its snout.

Ripping hooks!

He gives Sarah a high five, his hand black with blood.

Scotty asks Sarah to take their picture. She lifts the screen of her phone and Marko and Scotty pose behind the pig. Their teeth on show.

Ripping hooks.

Scotty steps around to admire them.

Your turn Sarah, cover of Bacon Babes for sure. But you got to take your top off for that.

Sarah glances at Marko, who shrugs.

If I had tits and I caught a boar like this …

Sarah looks at the pig like she might touch it again, her black nails shining like beetles, but she pulls off her shirt and hangs it over a branch. The strap of her bra is twisted. Marko stares at Sarah's fleshy breasts, one more bulky than the other, and Scotty grins like it's his birthday.

Awesome, he says and takes a photo of Sarah posing next to the boar. Awesome.

Marko looks at the web of stretch marks over Sarah's brown skin. She stands and laughs and pulls her shirt back on.

Never gone nude in the bush before, except for this one time —

Not every day you get a boar like this, Marko interrupts. You were great, the photos'll look great.

The cover, you reckon?

Sarah arranges her hair back around her shoulders. Marko stares at her breasts through the pink shirt.

With your looks, for sure.

Sarah smiles with her eyes.

What about my personality?

Come on lovebirds, Scotty calls, or we'll miss the weigh in.

The pigs are a pile of black, except where they've swelled in the sun and split their pink skin. Some of the guts remain, bloated like faces. The stink of sweet rot sits heavy on the air where Marko, Sarah, and Scotty line up around the outdoor bar to get beers. They watch their boar get weighed but it comes up small compared to some of the other fat bodies that still look alive, like they've just finished a feed. Scotty leans towards Sarah.

They stick them in water, get them all heavy — we should've done that. We should've done that, he tells Marko.

Marko sucks on the edge of his can.

With hooks like that who gives a fuck about the weight?

Too true. He lives for pigging, Scotty tells Sarah. Don't

try to get him excited about anything else. You want to give him a hard-on: stick a pig in the bed.

Sarah splutters her beer, and it sprays yellow.

The other piggers stand around to admire the hooks on their boar, now on the pile with the others, forever leaping with stiffened legs.

Those hooks, they say, you'll win for sure.

You should've seen Dingo go after him. She's small but she's a good fucken pigger.

Sarah here wasn't bad either.

Fuck off, Scotty, you weren't even there. But I meant you were good, too.

Marko glances over at Sarah. She smiles at him but not with her eyes. In the paddock beside them, little kids are throwing pig legs to see who can get the farthest. One girl watches the others, toying a severed leg with her bare foot. A woman sidles up to Sarah.

Haven't seen you here in ages. Where's your kid?

With my ex's mum.

I thought I saw him here before, says the woman and they both crane their necks to look through the crowd.

More people arrive, and the sweet pig smell is mixed with dust and sweat and beer. Marko loses Sarah between the swollen guts and pink bodies of Scotty and his mates. He stumbles through, looking at the women in jean shorts and black or pink polo shirts and blonde hair. He drinks two bourbon and colas, then takes his shirt off and loses it.

You'll do, he says to one woman.

What?

She's prettier than Sarah but she glares at him ugly.

Nothing.

Over by the bar, two of the lads push each other down and scramble in the dust. The blood paints their faces.

This is a family event, a man calls over the loud-hailer. For families.

The men stumble off to the car park to hit each other there. The man with the loud-hailer says they're going to judge the tusks, and Marko pushes towards the front. Their pig has been hauled out — just a head now that ends at the neck. Its big teeth look like they've been carved and shoved in a normal pig's mouth. They bring out another, a massive great thing with some serious tusks, and lay it in the line. The judges take their time with the measure at the mouths and Marko shuffles side to side. When they announce it, he nearly pisses himself. The hog head gets lifted up, and he props it on his bare shoulder with flies buzzing about his eyes and pig fur dried in solid clumps against his skin.

Wait up there's more of us.

Marko looks for them, unsteady with the weight of the boar. He can feel the fleas leaping from the dead pig to him. The man with the loud-hailer calls for Sarah and Scotty, but after a while they take the photo of Marko alone.

I must've been on the toilet.

Sarah is propped up against the bar. Marko's voice and body drag.

We fucken won. We'll split it three ways, right? You, me, and Scotty, when the money comes through. Because we fucken won.

He shows her the medal — a little metal pig on a wooden stand — and they order the pork roast and eat it at a table in the pub, away from the stench. Marko can still feel the fleas on him, and he scratches at his head. Across the beer garden Scotty is laughing hard at something. He catches Marko's eye and gives him the thumbs up. Marko shoves more pork in his mouth and turns back to Sarah.

About your ex, he says through a mouthful. I mean you can get over him if you want. But only if you want to. You know?

Sarah laughs around her beer.

I think I'll be right. I'm pretty confident. Being a mum, you have to be. For your kid's sake.

Oh, yeah. You like kids then?

Sarah laughs again.

I thought it was girls who asked that.

What?

I like kids, who doesn't?

Scotty. I mean he likes kids, he just wishes he doesn't have one.

Sarah glances over.

Maybe he hasn't met the right girl.

Marko launches out of his chair, and it tips and clatters back. He just makes it to the bushes around the corner of the pub to piss until he's empty. When he comes back around, he sees Sarah is still sitting alone. She's finished her beer and is rubbing lip balm on her lips. There's a loud roar from Scotty a few tables over and Marko flops into a chair beside him.

Marko's taken up with a shit-hot pigger, Scotty tells everyone.

Nah, she touched the pig.

Scotty leans forward. His smile splits his face in half.

She touched the pig?

Marko leaps up and starts humping the air, squealing. Scotty chokes on laughter. Marko cranes his neck to look at Sarah, who's half facing them and half not. He lands in his chair again.

Nah, just kidding. She just patted its nose or something.

Scotty paws Marko's face with his bloodied hands.

Oh, I love the little animals, he squeaks. Those piggers should be stabbed.

Marko laughs and pushes him away. He looks at Sarah again but her chair is empty.

Boars before whores, Scotty tells him and drains his beer.

Marko calls through the door of the empty ladies', where toilet paper is streamered over the cubicles. In the mirror the dried blood from the pig's head makes it look like half his face is coming off. He moves outside and peers through the dark to the pile of hogs. There's a figure hunched over, hand outstretched and teeth white in the shadows.

Leave her there, Marko says to himself, but he stumbles over.

Sarah doesn't move when he calls. He gets right up close but it's not her, it's just a dead sow, legs stiffened, black nails shining. The smell hits him. He makes it over to his pickup before he chucks up his guts in a rush. Dingo's eyes glint from the cage. He wipes his face and lets her out and shuts Rabies back in. Marko and Dingo weave back through the bodies of the hogs to the bar. But Scotty is gone, too. The music rattles over the empty chairs and tables. The little metal pig sits next to two half-finished beers — Sarah's lip balm is caked around the rim of one. Marko drains both, then walks off into the black. The pub lights bleed away behind him, and his knife beats a rhythm against his leg. The dog is beside him on the dirt. He starts to run.

TWENTY TWENTY

By the time Holly emerged from the house each day the drought was lighting the deck, scouring the dining table through the windows. Dan would say to her how great it would be at the beach, how it was a shame. The turmeric juices that Dan's mother served up were increasingly ignored against the force of the wheedling turning to sick frustration by Jac herself — a four-year-old in last year's bathers. The adult's acquiescence. The gathering of togs, gritty, snap-dried towels, and two puffy life rings that wouldn't have saved Jac from a rain shower but on which she depended for bravery, skill, and looks. On those mornings, Jac threw herself at Holly with the force of a wave. As if they hadn't gone yesterday and every day to the secret beach — looking both ways along the empty road and tiptoeing over someone's abandoned backyard to a thick scratchy path, and down to the cove with just enough sand and rock pools made warm in the sun. They lost time down there, often ran over lunch, and staggered back up to the house to eat nuts and cheese and snooze, their damp cold bathers wetting the couches.

'I'll go back down,' Holly told them: Dan, who had been drinking since they'd arrived; and her in-laws, Ruth and Matthew who, bow legged, appeared to straddle imaginary horses between the kitchen and the sitting room — pistols at dusk.

'It's dark.' Holly couldn't tell whether this was Dan's voice or her father-in-law's. A chill ran down her left shin.

'Dim,' she told one of them, rubbing her leg. She was still in damp togs herself, a long shirt. 'It's just dim, and I'll go down and be back.'

'Well. What about dinner?' Dan's mum. Another, much darker shape was crouched in the corner. Holly blinked, willing it to move — reveal itself. 'Holly?' Ruth asked.

'I was just doing salad. Put some lettuce out. Oil. Dan —'

'You'll never find them.'

'They glow.'

'Me, too,' announced Jac from the corner. 'I'm coming, too.'

'You stay here. Have a bath with ...' she felt like she was selecting for a sports team. Picked the only one likely to make it to the finish. 'Granny.'

The sky formed a dome over the house, like being inside a shell. Holly had already made this observation in the days before, and Dan had turned to her with pearly eyes, *yes, yes* — the way he did when he spotted a wisdom. Holly had wanted to repeat the statement to see his face do that again, but the last few evenings had been more like the inside of a lint-filled belly button. Now: a deep-sea shell with whorls of clouds scooping at the pink atmosphere. She wondered if she wished Dan was with her and looked up at the house deck. It was empty, the towels thrown haphazardly over the railing. Ruth and Matthew had bought the holiday place four-and-a-half years ago, and they used it all the time — they were practically locals — but the permanent residents mostly ignored them. There had been Christmas cards and drinks early on. Now it was hard to tell if anyone was living in the neighbours' houses, though their gardens were finicky and kept — one spiked with natives, the other with the suggestion of gnomes, scrim drawn. There were no kids outside here and making friends with these people who stayed locked inside was unlikely.

At that time of day, the cove was perfect — the sand stretched and crystallised, the water licking its way out and all the knee-gouging rocks exposed and navigable, forming rockpools. Holly turned to scramble for the house, intending to pluck her clean kid from the bath and restore her to the endless oceanic swim, but when she started back the empty beach moved. A man the colour of sand materialised a little way along from the path. Holly's voice caught in her throat. He was struggling with something.

The thing he held up against his face was so familiar Holly could have given birth to it. Hers, but also his. Her daughter's fluorescent-orange life preserver caught the end of the light. He had one wing to his mouth. The other was deflated beside him in the sand.

'That's mine,' Holly said, repeating one of Jac's favourite sayings. The age difference between her and the man was similar to that between mother and daughter. If she snatched the preserver, he didn't seem to notice. It was wet from him or the sea. Their fingers touched.

'We're not supposed to swim. It's against the rules.' Even down here she was reduced to the mantras. No sign stuck in sand, but it was written in the eyes of the locals. When the family ventured down to the small supermarket, they felt cast: rich escapees from the filthy city, come to use up the resources, infect the residents. *We're not really escaping — we're stuck!* Holly wanted to say. *And look: off-brand pasta!* But instead, they scuttled in and out. Matthew refused to go anymore after a snappy cashier had asked him to put on his mask.

'You need to wear it up over your nose, Dad,' Dan told him. 'At least for the look of it.'

'My sinuses,' Matthew muttered.

Holly clutched the preserver to her shirt and the man watched her keenly through milky eyes. *He's sick,* she thought despite herself. The skin on his legs. A starving elephant at a tourist tour. To reach the other preserver beside him, she had to get closer than she had to anyone other than her family in she-didn't-know-how-long. She edged forward and snatched at the float. Found herself holding her breath despite all the research Dan and his parents had done. The man smiled and waggled a finger at her.

'I'd better go back,' she told him. She, with the damning evidence of swimming in her hands now, not him. 'The rules.'

'If it wasn't for the out-of-towners, there wouldn't be a problem,' he said, using the sandbank behind him to struggle to a stand. So his household had their mantra, too. He was wearing the same kind of togs as muscle men from the 1950s. Thick and tight, cutting into the fragile flesh high up on his waist. The bathing suit version of bakelite. He took a step towards the flat sea.

'Swim?'

Holly pointed back up the weedy track, now cast in shadows. 'I have to —'

'They'll fit.' He raised his arms obediently, feet planted firmly. He was ancient. Demented. A saggy zombie. They lose all sense of boundary. Children and old people could be surprisingly strong.

The man lowered his arms. 'Well?'

'I'll just go wash these — get the sand off — and then we'll pop them on.' She hadn't intended for him to follow her. Just to wash his mouth off the preservers. Get away from the holding pattern of his bright egg-blue eyes. His trot was so heavy on the sand beside her she could feel its vibrations. The tide seemed even further out. At first lick, the cool water was so shallow her pinkie toe remained dry.

'Ah,' said the man, and slapped his chest. 'Swim?'

'I don't think we should swim. We're —'

'They don't want me to.' Holly looked around, half expecting to see the family he was attached to charging down the dim path. He beat his chest again. 'The old lungs. No good.'

The water up to their ankles. Now their shins.

'What's wrong with them?'

'Soft. Bunch of sooks.'

Holly laughed. 'Your *lungs*.'

This slapping of his chest was a thing. She wondered if it was to get something moving in there.

'Lung disease. They've got me wrapped in ... in ...'

'Cotton wool?'

'Yes.'

They both glanced back at the empty track. The chilly

water lapped around Holly's thighs now. The very texture
of the sea changed to something more like mercury in the
late light. She trailed the preservers in it, aware that certain
people would burn something a stranger had dribbled on.

'You'd better do it.' Holly handed him the ring. He
fumbled and dropped it in the water so it bubbled and
started drifting towards the sea bed. She plucked it out and
put it to her lips.

'That's right. Blow them up and we'll see what she's got.'

Was *she* the ocean, was *she* the little blow-up arm rings?
Or was *she* Holly? None of them had much energy. All were
tired. The news. The flu. The stillest water. The sun had set
enough that if fish or thoughts moved, Holly couldn't see
them. She tucked one of the rings under her arm, the other to
her mouth, as she had almost every day since they'd decided
to extend their long weekend indefinitely rather than to
go back to the mania of the closing city. One lockdown of
terrified case numbers — Jac's childcare run like a military
camp — and they weren't up for another. Holly had bought
the blow-up rings at the gift shop to convince Jac of her new
and suddenly smaller life. The old man caught Holly's eye
and she showed her teeth around the nozzle and filled it
with enough air to give it some structure. They stopped at
waist deep and the man held out his arm again so that Holly
could thread it on. She pushed it over his bony wrist. She
was being brusque.

'Atta girl,' he said, nodding with approval. To blow the
thing up she needed to get close again. Police. Helicopters
with spotlights. No one else appeared on the distant beach.
Maybe this is how doctors felt about bodies. Ignore the
obvious discomfort of the patient — it's just a thing to fix.

Not that the man seemed uncomfortable. Perfectly happy to wait while she clamped her teeth around the nozzle right next to his skin and filled the plastic with air. One of those men who is used to women doing things for him. Some executive. Or a farmer.

'What did you do? For work?' she asked, wading around with the second ring to the other raised arm. 'I mean unless you still —'

'Teacher. Primary School.' He pointed in the vague direction of the small school on the other side of the town.

'Really?'

He gave a sharp nod. 'Musicals were my thing.'

'Right.' He probably wasn't a musical teacher at all. He was probably making it all up at this point.

'I'm an influencer,' Holly tried.

'Not very even.' He frowned at the right ring, which was decidedly smaller than the left. Holly gave it another blast of air and sealed it up.

'We have filters for all that.' She smiled — wanting him to be in on the joke — but he was swinging his arms back and forth. Squeezing the rings nervously. 'Actually, I'm just in logistics. Sustainable packaging. It's all gone online which makes it' — he wasn't listening — 'pretty redundant.'

It was a surprise when he launched himself in. There was so much of him that the still water became turbulent. The plastic rings did nothing. Dan and his parents had done a course over at the main beach one summer on how to recognise the signs of drowning. They were always doing courses together on animal husbandry or horticulture or self-defence. The water safety course was from the time before — so distant that Holly wondered, increasingly, if she'd imagined it. There were a lot of facts. Apparently, some people didn't look like they were drowning, you might think they were waving or just having a nice time in the water. This man was submerged and, when he came up, spluttering. Holly reached forwards into the cold space between them and hauled him up facing away from her. She hooked her arms under his like she would with her daughter.

'Hello,' she said in his ear. He was light in the water. Smelled of brine and tea. He immediately stopped thrashing and let Holly and the weak floatation rings and salty water support him. No, not used to women doing things for him, thought Holly, used to trusting people. 'How's that?'

'I'm swimming,' he said.

'Hope you don't catch a cold.' It sounded more ominous than she'd intended.

He twisted a little in the water. 'Do you think we'll know it's coming?'

'What's coming?'

'The Chinese plague. What's it called?'

'It's just a flu. My husband's a doctor. A kind of doctor. And he says he's never met anyone with the coronavirus. He completely cured my father-in-law's gout. You should see him about your lungs.'

Back at the house the family had the lights on, Jac dried and absorbed in Lego. Beside the stove Holly found an easy dinner of salmon, salad, and broccoli, with plenty left for her to pick at.

'Did you get them?' Dan asked. Holly picked up a wedge of fish and used it to point towards the back door where the life rings lay in a salty heap. 'What took you so long?'

'There was an old man at the beach. We talked.'

Dan nodded encouragingly. 'Keeping it normal. Helping people to understand they don't need to be afraid.'

Keeping it normal in their strange isolation was Dan's primary motivation these days. His homeopathy practice had become virtual, and he couldn't send out the prescriptions, but there were an awful lot of enthusiastic client calls. Holly's job had been whittled down to a few hours of desultory clicking; team meetings with her camera turned off.

'Jacqueline's got a bit of a cold,' Ruth announced. 'A sore throat,' she mouthed, nodding at Jac. 'A bit hot.' They peered at Jac, who did look flushed. Eyes glazed as she leaned back against Grandpa's legs, content to watch Dan make the rest of the castle. Her skin, Jac told them solemnly, did feel itchy but Holly eyed the lolly jar for the cause of this. Grandma seemed a little red-lolly hyped herself.

'What's the story, sweetheart?' Ruth asked now. Jac's heavy-lidded eyes opened a little wider at the mention of a story.

'She means how are you feeling?' Holly added.

'I'm feeling … hot.' Jac looked at the circle for approval.

'A cold.' Dan put down the Lego and peered at his daughter. 'Arsenic album.'

'You're not giving her arsenic,' Matthew said.

'Calm down, Matty, it's one of his medicines,' Ruth said. 'Remember how he fixed your gout?'

•

The morning rose again and Holly was in the kitchen wondering aloud how long it would take for the big supermarket in the next town to deliver when Dan told her that surely they could just duck down the street to the grocery store. He opened the cupboard beside her and surveyed the scant shelves of instant soups, four-bean mix, cereal, and lollies.

'There's rules,' Holly told him. 'If she's got those symptoms.'

Dan wrapped his arms around her from behind. 'And we're following the rules. We're staying put in the town. Wearing our masks. Taking our vit C.' His hands slid down her stomach to the waist of her pants. They had a bedroom upstairs with a great view right down to the secret beach, but it also overlooked the septic tank. Sex had never smelled so off-putting. If Dan was frustrated, he was midnight snacking his way through and that explained their diminished supplies. They were low on tins and pasta and there were no tissues for Jac, who was using toilet paper to blow her nose and the roll itself as a giant bangle.

'We do need to stock up,' Holly said. Dan nodded approvingly into her shoulder and Holly felt the love coming off him — some of it for her, some for the idea of more supplies.

'You can stay here with her? I'll get changed ...'

'Sure you don't want company up there?' Dan released her and wiggled his eyebrows. Holly sniggered. Maybe a good fuck *would* be the ticket. But Dan had already grabbed a few salted cashews and wandered off into the lounge room to find his charge.

•

In the end, all five set out to the grocery store. The adults a little battle-scarred after Jac had yelled the house down about never never never staying home with Grandpa and Dad. They left with shopping bags but not quite enough masks, and decided on ice creams for the way home. Matthew said the masks they sold in a little box by the door were a rip off so Holly waited outside holding the scooter and the shopping while Jac, Dan, and his parents disappeared into the gloom. Holly ran her eyes over the car park, looking for a friendly face — or any face. People scuttled in and out, heads down, expressions covered. A car parked carefully under a tree contained the old man. He was pressed up against the glass and someone had left a gap in the window like he was the family dog. Holly ducked her head to the man's level, called hello.

'Hello,' he said. It wasn't clear if he recognised her or not.

'Nice to see you. It's Holly.'

'What?'

Holly got closer to the glass. 'Holly.'

The man smiled politely — *he doesn't remember* — but rolled the window down further to stick out a hand. Holly shook it, the strong bony grasp. The man nodded at the beach, a slick of blue at the end of the shimmering street. 'Swim?'

Holly laughed. It was still impossible to tell if he knew her or invited every stranger. The man laughed, too, and they were like this, clutching hands and grinning, when someone shouted *excuse me*. Holly dropped the man's hand like she'd been about to steal it and turned to see another family: the masked mum and the dad around her age, the tween kid.

'Do we know you?'

It was funny: Holly could tell just from people's eyes that they were unfriendly. She didn't need their frowning mouths.

'We've met.' Holly gestured at the old man, whose gaze was fixed on the sea. She could feel herself panicking, breathless. Jac's cold was setting in.

'What were you thinking?' The family frowned into the car.

'We're just talking.'

'He's immunocompromised. Are you crazy?'

'That's because he hides inside all day.' Holly followed the dad around the car. He climbed into the driver's seat as angrily as one can into a Barina. 'It's all a bit overblown though, right?' Holly tried as he closed the door. 'Flu is normal. We don't need to be frightened.'

'You can just fuck off with your conspiracies,' the man said to her, starting the car.

'Christopher!' the woman shouted from the passenger seat. The tween was giggling, but the old man didn't seem to notice. Holly tried to catch his eye as they drove away. At the corner she thought she saw his big hand waving through the back window. Her own family emerged from the shop and tore off their face masks. Jac jumped around trying to get her ice cream. Ruth brandished a newspaper.

'More fearmongering.'

'I don't want to see. I get it in meetings at work. It's making me crazy.'

Ruth waved it again. 'Have to stay informed.'

'It's good to know what they're saying,' Dan said to everybody. *Why don't you just marry you mum then?* The thought popped into Holly's head before she could banish it. Holly had to at least be more mature than Jac, who was perched on the bench outside the shop, eating her ice cream pretty neatly.

What she said instead was, 'We should go to the secret beach. The salt water will be good for Jac's nose.' She was trying to appeal to Dan's sensibilities, but his face fell a bit. He'd been giving horse rides in the lounge room all morning between clients. He likely wanted, as he did most afternoons out here, to have a whiskey and catch up on some articles while Jac watched *Peppa Pig* and Ruth gaped at the neighbours disinfecting their shopping with spray bottles in the yard next door.

So it was just Holly and Jac who went hand-in-hand straight from the shops. A snatch of freedom in their diminished world. They would swim in their underwear. They would dry in the sun. Her daughter had the step of someone for whom most of the wishes of life had just come true without her even voicing them. How exhausting, Holly thought, to be four years old and constantly having to ask for what you want. For your future to be decided by others.

'What do you see for your future?' she asked Jac suddenly. It was a question from Holly's childhood and came out at odd angles to their relationship, but Holly saw Jac find a familiar fold to slot it in.

'The beach!' she yelled. Holly hurried her on past a family group of intense shoppers — hard to tell if they were frowning at the maskless Holly and Jac or just at the world.

'What else though?' She couldn't stop it, now that it was out. She tugged Jac's hand a little so the girl looked up. 'What do you really think about the future?'

'Is it a bike?'

Holly tried to smile reassuringly. 'You've got a bike. It's just in the city. I mean what do you want, you know, from life.'

'Oh. A Slurpee.' Jac tripped over a lumpy bit of grass and recovered herself to ask, 'What's a Slurpee?'

'It's a ... a drink. You had one at Tui's birthday.' The streets were baking now. Jac's ice cream had dripped all down her arm. She held it dutifully out to the sun, not eating it anymore but not dumping it on the street either. There was something so sad, Holly thought, about an upside-down ice cream cone. When she and Dan had first moved in together down a London alley, they saw, one summer dawn on their return from a club, a box of cheap wine with an ice cream cone upturned on top of it. Dan had said 'someone had a party' and stared when Holly cried and cried, because what Dan has seen as a celebration, she had viewed as the loneliest scene.

'Mummy.'

'Yes?'

'What do you think about in the future time?'

'Mmm. I think your dad will fix your cold. And ... then I think we'll hop on a plane for a real holiday all the way over the ocean to see my mummy and daddy. How about that?'

They had arrived at the empty yard that led to the secret beach. Holly lifted Jac up over the gorse of the scratchy path, arms extended so as not to mash them both with ice cream, and dumped her onto the beach. The tide was up. Beaches follow their own time, honouring moons, not clocks. Holly wondered if children had some inbuilt sense of the tides — having been so recently in the womb. That's how she could explain it all to Jac. The little girl was jiggling impatiently, her ice cream now just a cone brimming with slop. Holly took it and nestled it into the sand, pulled down Jac's shorts and led her to one of the closer rock pools. While her daughter gingerly washed, Holly felt a presence behind her and knew it was the elderly gent. She looked back to nothing.

'I'm clean,' Jac announced, her face still smeared. She wanted to play running in and out of the waves, not to paddle in the cool frothing water.

'Should we swim?' Holly echoed the old man. Jac squealed again, escaping from a trickling wave. Holly watched her and didn't watch her from her ankle-deeper position. Her daughter never let up. Never flailed on the performative squeal as the waves rushed back towards her. She's keeping oceanic time, Holly realised. She can just do it, and I have to stand here with my feet buried in the sand contemplating it. The waves caught on something. A collection of shells and stones that had washed up in a way that seemed purposeful. Some sort of installation. Gods in a department meeting.

'Look at this!' Holly called to Jac, and the girl hobbled dutifully across the sand and rocks. Holly held her by the shoulders to show how the rocks changed colour every time a wave broke over them.

'This is the beauty of the natural world. We don't need to be all doom and gloom.' She immediately felt embarrassed. It was sort of against the rules to talk to their daughter about all that. She was four and should be thinking about how to jump the highest. 'But what do you think, Jac?'

The girl checked that her audience of one was ready, backed up like a small salmon truck and — ignoring Holly's warnings — lifted her feet and ran at the sharp collection. Wailed the quiet streets all the way home.

•

Their attention turned to Matthew, who suddenly went pale and had to take to bed. Two hours later, they found him shivering in navy-blue underwear in the hall and put him back under the quilt. They stood in the carpeted hallway outside the big double room with its whirring pedestal fan and whispered to each other. Holly leaned in the doorway and watched Dan administer remedies — *Atropa belladonna, Rumex, Anas barbariae* — for the severity of the flu. For Dan and his parents, it was serious. They shivered and sweated and said that their heads slammed with pain and one night they debated taking further action for Ruth — so breathless was she. Dan talked heroically from his own bed about breaking out of the town to get to one of his colleagues, an apothecary with a complete set of remedies only an hour away. Holly's cold passed like a wind that made her sneeze a lot. She sat by her mother-in-law and wriggled hot wheat packs under her aching legs.

'I got you these,' Holly told Ruth while Dan and Matthew were out watching a movie on the couch, leaving the big squashy double bed to Ruth. Holly popped a couple of paracetamols from a packet hidden in her pocket and put them in Ruth's hand, who giggled and accepted the glass of water to wash them down.

'Holly,' Ruth said.

'Just take them.' Holly blew her nose. 'No one thinks a fever is good for you.'

'Did you — and it's okay if you did — did you do one of those coronavirus-19 remedies on Jac? The bleach or the other one? Do you think it's real?'

'Of course I didn't. Of course I don't.'

Ruth tried to sit up, but became breathless so slumped

down again. 'It's fine if you believe it. Your parents are doctors.'

'They're psychiatrists.'

'I just want to know,' Ruth panted.

'I wouldn't be here if I did. I'd be off with the handwringers in the city. You've got that nasty flu that's going around and anyway we can't trust those men to look after you properly, even Doctor Dan.'

'Yes.' Ruth looked out the window to where the boats on the cove were twinkling their little lights. She drew a difficult breath. 'I really don't feel so good.'

Holly could smell the septic system even through her blocked nose — it really did come all the way up to Holly and Dan's bedroom. If Holly tucked her phone in her bra and stood on the bed, she could push the window all the way open, sling a leg over and slide through. She crouched on the green tank for a moment, taking in the layout of the sheer drop down to the driveway and past the balcony on one side, and to a tangled layer of dense green on the other — impossible to tell how deep it was. The ringtone reached out.

'Is she breathless?' Holly's dad asked. He was in an earlier timezone and was panting himself.

'You're on your walk.'

'I'm up the stairs to look at Dev's email.'

'Yes, breathless.'

'Okay, let's see what he said. Fever?'

'Yes.'

Able to talk? Yes. Does she make sense? Sense? When she talks — or is she confused? No, lucid. Any chest pain?

No. Lips blue? Unable to stay awake? No, no.

'I'm just on chat with him — ha, he's asking if we can play virtual golf!'

'Dad.'

'He said to watch her then and check back in the morning. But call a health line for goodness sakes, Holly. You're not in a cult.' Two nights earlier, Dan and Matthew had called Healthline dial-a-data-collection. Holly imagined hauling Ruth out the bedroom window to get her to a hospital — the old girl would probably be up for it.

Dramatic music filtered up from the lounge room, the movie reaching its finale. Down on the secret beach, a figure appeared. No, a rock. A figure — it moved. From the shape, it had to be him. The undergrowth like carpet — Holly relied on this now as she dropped down onto it, feeling the cords give and bear her. On her hands and knees she slithered through it, sinking into pits of thinner growth and being caught again. She felt her mask slip out of her pocket and fall into the unknown space below — grateful that her phone was tucked back in her bra. Her nose dripped. She wiped it on her forearm as she picked her way along the path. Down on the beach they grinned at each other ruefully. The man held out his arms and Holly hesitated.

'Swim?' he asked, and she realised he was gesturing for the life rings, which were in the house laundry.

'We're going alone tonight.'

'Alone together?'

Holly smiled — a wisdom! They made their way towards the water in their clothes. The man seemed unsteady, wheezing into the moonlight. Between breaths he told her how he taught musical theatre by updating the scores with the 'good' music of the sixties and seventies.

'Beatles or Stones?' Holly asked him as they reached the edge.

He turned to look at her, eyes now the grey and green of ocean rocks. 'That's a stupid question.'

They walked into the water in silence. Mid-tide, but with a sturdy drop into darkness that caused him to stumble and Holly to grab his bony elbow. The chilly water bled up Holly's jeans.

'The Stones don't do anything worth repeating,' he told her sternly as he took his elbow back. Holly sneezed. 'You can't believe in them.'

They were up to their waists. Holly crouched down a little so the cold water clawed her chest. Back up on the beach, streetlights flickered warnings through the trees. She swished her arms. The man did the same.

'They're fun, but there's no story, no follow through. They're not saying anything.' A short wave slapped his shoulder and got in his mouth.

'Try kicking,' Holly said. He coughed, slapped his chest, then stuck out his impossibly long legs. The motion made him lose his footing on the sand below and he sank under. She lost him beneath the foam. Reaching in, she could feel him — not thrashing around like she'd expect, but very still. Adrenal strength threaded through her arms as she grabbed a part of him and hauled him up on the next small wave. He was fine, grinning even, but his skin felt hot. He breathed out — Holly couldn't smell him.

'What do you want?'

'If you could just help me,' he said.

'We should ...'

'Just your arm under there.'

So he did remember. Not cuckoo after all. She tucked her arms beneath his again and felt his big heart beating in its cage. She recalled what Matthew had told her about blue whale hearts being the size of golf carts. What sort of person compares living organs to rich person vehicles, Holly had wanted to know? But Dan's dad was partial to a bit of golf so she had tucked that piece of knowledge away until now, whale heart, beating.

'You can go,' the man told her.

'What?'

'You go on back now, I'll take it from here.'

'I don't think ... but you can't swim.'

He twisted. They'd drifted out, Holly realised, neither of them touching the ground, Holly suspending them there with regular safety kicks. The water was murky, impossible to see through.

'I'm swimming now!' He started to swish away from her. Then, 'This is swimming!' For a second she imagined him launching into a slow, powerful overarm, winging out to sea. Then he started to slip, and she knew he would keep sinking. She got him back, her arm under his chin.

'I'll punch you in the face,' she found herself saying, 'if you don't stay still.' After that, he was motionless, skin burning, until they were back to touch-sand and all the way up to waist level. He was morose once beached. Coughing shallowly. Holly's hair stuck to her cheeks, her jeans dragging damply at their cuffs. They made their way up to a small hillock of grasses by Holly's track and stood hugging themselves. He had some other path through the trees to get home.

'You asked me what I want,' he said, his shirt pasted in clumps to his body.

Holly's teeth began to chatter. 'I didn't mean that.'

'Better out there than in some hospital with the rest of them.'

'Don't be ridiculous. You're not going to die.' She thought of the breathless woman she'd left up at the house.

'Dad always said I should hold my breath if I found myself in the drink. There wasn't time to learn.' He waved his hands in a swimming motion, a drowning motion.

Holly looked back up at the dim track — it seemed so lonely. 'Can you hold your breath now?'

He tried, but started to cough.

279

Did they look like cows?

I guess so, Con. Shrunken sky cows with wings and blazed chests. And beaks.

What's a beak?

It's a dreamy sort of a question. A question for off times, shovel leaning, inside from too much rain.

A beak, Con, is what a bird has.

What's a bird? I mean, you've said what a bird is. Avio —

Avian —

Avian, all that. But what is a bird.

A bird isn't anything.

Connie climbs off the couch to right the handle of a bucket and to haul it — nuggety little thing — across the room. The rain hangs from the ceiling crack like a string of beads and scatters over the floor. Connie would more know a string of beads than a bird. We have beads. I used to see bird carcasses around, but their hollow flying bones are no good for swamping. The floods. What was left of the chickens — those mass graves — has been washed away. She opens the door, crosses the wet porch, and tips. The water from the bucket sloshes into the water channelling past the steps of the house.

How high? I call. What about the cows?

Um. The milking shed. And it's up to our first step. The cows are on the island.

She puts the bucket back — the leak in the ceiling now a bony beat on the plastic base. Connie's face when she gets on the couch again.

I'll do it, I tell her, from now on.

Can you say about the other animals?

It's too upsetting.

Come on.

I take a breath. There were lizards — reptiles. One old as anything.

She doesn't ask if a lizard looks like a cow, but how else to describe it?

You know how our feet get when we're unstucking the cows? I say.

Bare foot? Wrinkled. Old.

That's a lizard. That's tuatara. Was. Old as anything. Older than ... Why mention dinosaurs? Pointless ... older than 279.

Bye 279.

When the oldest one slipped and fell in the drink, we took off our gumboots and waded in. I wasn't worried for us — the tide wasn't much, and with Connie eight already and so sensible — but 279 was embedded and lowing in the sucking mud. The rain stopped for a bit; the cow quietened, looked around, then gathered her haunch muscles and heaved, swimming her forelegs for solid ground — it seemed hopeful. I could almost have joined her without getting trampled. Out of habit, I glanced at the sky, expecting to see a bird where only clouds flocked. It rained so hard then I did fear for Connie. We withdrew up the hill to the porch. The cow slipped again, went under.

Bye 279, said Connie.

But there were nightmares and a kicked-over bucket, a refusal to eat the beans that we don't really have enough of to refuse. Next flood, we got the big headphones and connected her to my phone, and I found a quicker way to deal with it. Now Connie's staring at her feet, a bit pruned, calling them lizards.

Why are there cows? I mean, why only them? Do you love them the most?

Outside, one of them calls through the rain. There are no other sounds. Lowing and water.

What will you play? I ask Connie.

Her eyes go blank. What should I? I mean. How loud?

The loudest.

I wait until the guitar tins through the room. I honestly downloaded that hair metal once as a joke. Second step. Don't drop the gun. Toes dipping into the water like ducks used to drink. The cows have found the island, but their swamp-weakened hooves have not. Twenty-two of them pressed like at a cattle yard. One slips and can't make it back up the bank. I've got a good eye.

WHAT WE DO

The last hours of May. The air is sticky, no moon, and we've been at that bar with the generator. Outside, because of the power outages, there are people in the motorbike-lit streets.

We catch a tuk tuk. Our voices throw over the dim parade — Kings have been there, Charles de Gaulle has been there, the Khmer Rouge have been there ... but a plastic crack like a giant toy gun interrupts us: the sound one motorbike makes when it hits another.

Then there's one man writhing like agony over the road. And there's the other man he hit facedown. The slow dimming strobe of his bike lights up his blue jeans and his oiled black hair. He's oddly tall and handsome like that.

He's dead.

People run along the Quay. Their flip-flops echo in a strange silence where there are no screams, no sirens, but our quiet argument: What do we do? What do we do? We've been at that bar with the generator. We've been to the temples and the killing fields and the bars and the pool. What do we do?

We hang over the back of the moving tuk tuk like kids on a bus and watch the divide. We watch the asphalt slide beneath us. How soft the road looks then.

SITE

Nobody is asleep at this time, but April is. When she wakes, she is in half-light and watches the sky coming in through the window. The whole day has been the same. A nothing sky fading into sea. Sitting up a little further in bed she can see the ship still out there on the water. Closer now. It arrived in the harbour a week ago when she started the painting. A brick against the sky. It has been growing ever since. She has tried to sketch it but when she looks at it head-on, it evaporates. She gives up and turns back to the new work. Now the ship sits like a block of flats halfway between her and the horizon. The view from her house is a broad slice of ocean. The ship takes up half of it.

The last thing she did worth hanging is there on the wall. 'A picture of fruit in a brown frame'. Colours that show the bright tones of a summer almost three years earlier. Just after she and Andi split. A self-portrait. Not really about anything, just a reflection of that week. Like a diary entry. Or a blurred photograph. She has told people this, maybe the same people twice, but it's important. It won second prize, and people said it should have been first. But it didn't sell and that was a mystery to everyone. Her new pieces haven't been picked up — the use of ochre is edgy, transgressive, problematic. The gallery notes: 'We'd value a return to your previous concepts.' They don't look good in this light.

She lives in the old tourist centre, which came semi-furnished. Over time she's removed the receipt stubs and the lobby chairs, the signs pointing to the bathroom in one direction and the site of cultural significance in the other. Now she sets it up like a gallery, her new painting at its centre. She sees Andi in front of it, beside the roaring fire, drinking the pinot he might still like. The man who can deliver the wood says he only takes cash, so she pulls on sneakers and jogs with a backpack down to the shops to get money. Stands rubbing her bank card against her cheek at the general store, imagining Andi squeezing her calf in his dry designer's hands, drawing a line along the muscle.

'I remember these legs.'

The owner scans the items without looking at them.

'Ship's big today,' she comments — pushing through bread, turpentine, tampons, with her eyes on the sea. 'See it from the site, can you?' April nods in reply and watches the grey vessel. 'We used to take the kids there. Shame. You'd get a marvellous view, though.' The store owner pauses mid-scan, staring out. 'I can't stand the colour. Like blood.'

'Blood? Grey blood?' A heavy cloud about to rain, if anything. The owner peers at the ship again, then at April, as though she's the one making no sense.

•

April runs hard back up the hill, the shopping bashing her back, and feels a wave of nausea at the top to find Andi's car already there. But it's not his. Two tourists gingerly lift the drop cloth she's draped over the tourist sign to stop them coming to her door.

'Are you closed?'

April nods. She can spy the wood truck in the driveway, where the man has dumped the half tonne, not in the garage like she asked.

'When are you open?'

'We're not. I mean, it's private now.'

'How are we supposed to do the cultural trail if we can't see the culture?' They say it more to each other than to her, climbing back into their Andi-car. The wood guy has wandered away to stand in the front yard where they used to start the guided tour. A few logs carved into rough tables and chairs so people could sit and eat their packed lunches before heading down the track. The man is staring through the trees to where the ship floats. Its detail should be more apparent now that it's closer, but the entire thing is grey to the point of being two-dimensional.

'Couldn't upend the trailer in the garage,' the man explains below dark glasses. April moves to stand beside him, craning for doors or levels on the ship, a sign of someone on board, but there's nothing.

The man squints, mutters, 'Why'd they paint it so bright?' and turns away.

When he has gone April moves the wood by hand, at first lifting slices of the pine and heaving them towards the back of the garage, where they splinter and split. Easier to burn. Then the heavy chunks of redwood, hugging each log to her chest and eyeing the insects running wild inside the bark beneath her chin. One piece has chopped so neat the surface seems planed and sanded to a smooth fine grain — she grunts it inside. Falls back against the pillow again, wiggles her fingers. Tests her back, stretching it to a click, but it doesn't hurt. She's lucky, she reflects, and looks out again at the ship. Andi said that he would be there after five. Probably six. *I'm busy, but you're important. A priority.*

The shower is hot as hell — steam gushing up as the water comes down. April's shampoo and April's soap. She cleans the plughole with her big toe. Scrubs the wood dust out from under her nails. Runs the water hotter over her stomach. From that angle, it looks bigger, distended. She and Andi had talked about babies before they stopped talking. There was still time, even if her doctor said that a thirty-six-year-old pregnancy would be geriatric. Out of the shower, she tips upside down to blow-dry her hair, and watches a watercolour line of blood winding its way down the skin of her inner thigh.

Her phone might have played the Andi ringtone while she was in the shower, but it hasn't. She puts in a tampon and pulls on a thin purple jumper that looks better without a bra, loose pants. She doesn't bother with underwear. The place is bare. She could see how it made a good tourist spot, rimmed with windows facing the water — trees on either side obscuring the site of cultural significance, down the overgrown path and scooping around to a cave over the water

where women gave birth for millennia. The council don't
know what to do with the site. They took away the landlord's
tourist license and made it free, but it was vandalised. In
the meantime, the landlord rents the place cheap to April.
She's picked her way down the old tourist track to stare into
the cave, trying to picture Wadawurrung women there, but
all she can see is herself, pale and brutal in the entry way. A
book about Western Desert style at the art supply shop she
works at in the city gave her the idea to capture it in dots.
She practiced on the note pad in between serving customers.

'That's a bit wrong, April!' Her workmate laughed. But he
was a nineteen-year-old cultural studies student who thought
her hoop earrings were inappropriate. 'Western Desert style
wouldn't be used around here.' He had more to say about the
development of abstract, naturalistic, and line movements.
April focused on the dots. She still doesn't know what they
mean — she's only part way through the book — but she
likes the way they gather and swim on the canvas in browns,
purples, and creams, growing darker as she reaches the depths
of the cave. She imagines herself as one of the women, giving
birth in there, painting thicker and faster until something
stops her, presses in too hard and almost ruins the work.
Problematic. Beyond it all, the ship moves. She shoves her
paints and canvases in drawers or piles them in the spare
room. She breathes, fingers things, adjusts them, and lights
the oil burner to make it all smell, then blows it out again.

April is too tired to sleep and too tired to be awake. She's
wired on time. Stands in the kitchen with her hands on a
mug, waiting for the kettle to boil. Her arms are sore from

the wood. He must be only moments away. Must be lost. It's the first time he'll be in her world. Usually, they meet at a hotel. Once they met at his place, after he fought with Sophia and she left for a week. Andi and April had familiar sex on the new chair in his lounge room, trying not to tense whenever a car swung its lights through the windows — a high, white beam over their bodies and the room. Her phone begins to ring — the guitar riff Andi wrote for her back in the day, although he'd dedicated the song to Sophia on the album.

'Where are you?' she asks.

'Bloody stuck in traffic at the moment. I'm still in the city.'

'The city?' April looks over at the clock on the wall. He'll be an hour. Maybe more.

'Yeah, I had another meeting with The Cyan Group — big, big job. Diversity etcetera. No, but they're good blokes. We're hiring another guy to handle the accounts.'

'And you care about diversity.'

'Um. Yeah. Since Dad was nearly arrested leaving Tirana? Mum was pregnant with me? Jesus, April —'

His parents. The intensity of family dinners. The fishy Albanian food. 'I was joking. I mean. I've started a new piece. You'll love it, Andi. It's cultural.' He doesn't answer. 'When will you be here?'

He makes a hissing sound. The best possible outcome sound. Wherever he is, a car honks and then another.

'Well, I've got to drop some stuff off with the client and then if I get a good run ... a few hours? By seven?'

'Okay. Can't wait to see you.'

'It's just a pity I can't stay the night.'

'You can't?'

'I've got the plumbers coming, and Sophia. She'll be back then.'

'I thought she wasn't coming back until the afternoon ...' April can't stop her tone.

'She's not, April, but I still have to do things. To be there.' To look like he has been there.

'I wish you could stay. I always love waking up with you,' she says instead.

'You can go to sleep with me. I'll watch you sleep, and I won't leave until late.'

'What if I don't sleep?'

'You will. I'll tire you out.'

'How will you do that?' She puts the smile back in her voice, weighs it, and he laughs in response, high and breathless like he does with her.

'I'll show you soon. Seven. Eight at the latest.'

She thinks she hears him outside. Hears a car door slam. Footfalls on the back deck. The scent of him in her mouth, already there. But when she goes to the window, there's just the straggle of wattle blocking her view, the driveway bare but for the leaves. She goes outside anyway, her socks on the cold dirt. Maybe he parked at the start of the drive or out on the street? But there's no one. Just the rush of wind picking up right at the very tops of the trees. On a certain angle, it cries through the cave, and April feels the strange longing, the strange rage. If she could harness it on canvas, make it her own. Out in the bay the water is darkening. The grey ship closer. Its grey even greyer on the dusk of the water.

A dangerous time to drive, and what about boating? She imagines she can hear the waves falling against the hull, but it might only be the rocks at the cave's entrance.

A car comes down the road, large and yellow with headlights like moons, even though it's still light. Not Andi's. The kind of car the neighbours drive — practical. It pulls into the driveway next door, and April can see her neighbours sitting in there. Not speaking. Lisa and ... Tam? They wave at April, their smiles tight with argument.

'Funny day,' says Tam across the small fence that separates them as she hauls the baby from the backseat. The child kicks at the empty air. 'The forecast said rain, but it hasn't come. I've checked every site. It was definitely supposed to rain.'

'I thought it would, too,' replies April. And then, because she feels like she's only heard Andi's voice for days, in her head and on her phone, 'It's still cold at night. I had to order more wood.' Andi's body stretched out in front of the fire. She'll tell him about her new life, her friends next door. How great they are.

'Very cold,' replies Tam, bouncing the baby distractedly. 'By the way, what colour would you say that ship was out there?'

'Don't,' Lisa fumes, coming around the side of the car with too many supermarket bags.

'I'm just asking. It's "April", isn't it? Right. April, what colour does that ship look to you?'

'You don't have to answer,' Lisa tells April, glaring at Tam.

'Grey,' April answers. 'Dark grey.' Grey isn't a colour — the first thing she ever learnt about paint. Tam hoots and lifts the baby up and down so that it laughs, too.

'Grey!' she repeats.

'It doesn't matter what colour the bloody thing is,' Lisa hisses, and then smiles tightly at April. 'She won't stop talking about it.'

'You two are both insane,' laughs Tam. 'Grey! My wife here thinks it's purple. Like a bruise. Won't look at the thing, will you, baby?'

'But it *is* grey,' April says quietly, standing on her tiptoes to see. They would get a better view from their place, a bit higher, closer to the beach, not so many trees.

'Bullshit,' Tam says jovially, and Lisa turns and stomps inside, her miniature arms weighed down with handles. 'It's bright blue. Look at it! Same colour as the water. I can hardly see it even now. Blends in.' She steps a bit closer. 'That's what really gets me — how it disappears all the time, but I can feel it, you know? And then at night the moon picks it up and it's just there glowing. Lisa can't sleep, she says, with me pacing around. She won't look at it. Like a bruise, she reckons. Makes her want to cry.' Tam spins the baby in a precise sort of flip. He giggles uncontrollably. Something moves on the broad deck of the ship. A figure, then another.

April's socks are covered with sticks and leaves that track through the house. She isn't going to be wearing them when Andi arrives. She'll be barefoot. Natural. Different to Sophia, who makes up just to go to the shops, Andi has said. It seems so long ago that they were together. She knows his life in a noisy apartment right in the city, their soul-grinding jobs — April at the bank; Andi mining — fighting even more than they fucked. Now in snippets of half marathons and guitar. Freelancing. Sophia. All those spaces in between.

How they'd been introduced to each other again at that ridiculous dinner, a snort and a hooded wink from Andi, questions about things they knew intimately.

'Where did you grow up, April?'

'Inner south.'

'Ah, fancy girl.'

'Not *my* school.'

'Still. Bet you've been to the Great Ocean Road.'

She smiled at the memory. 'I have, yes.'

'Did you have a good time there?'

'I did. Camping. It was very memorable.'

Andi's high snigger. 'Go on.'

'I stayed up all night.'

'Couldn't sleep?'

He was trying to make her blush. She leaned towards him. 'Too noisy.'

He laughed in earnest. The other guests looked down the table at them, curious.

It isn't really night yet — just late in the day. The birds are still out and the sun, which never properly appeared, still shines from somewhere behind a hill of clouds. The trees are blowing and bending away from the house in a spring wind that moves them in a ripple all the way down to the ocean. She watches the birds chasing each other desperately through the leaves. Spring: such a barbaric season. It makes her see Andi everywhere. On her couch, in her kitchen. She puts her old cup in the sink and gets out a new one, boils the jug. Leans back over the bench and sighs — the way she does with him. Her body. That Andi loves. He has said so:

'I love those breasts, I love those thighs.' And April returns
it, 'I love you inside me, I love ...' That's when it's allowed
— when it's physical. She's sure they're saying more. When
he arrives, the light will be fading, and he'll just be able to
make out the water. He'll grin and point at the ship and
tell her what colour he sees. Then it won't be grey anymore.
April will see it through his eyes. Her painting, so opaque,
will become clear. Lit up like the top of the ship — now
glowing with flickering lamps. She can see the ship from
the corner of her eye — straight on, she doubts it's even
there. But while the ship looks modern, a cargo tanker or a
warship — April doesn't really know — the people on the
deck are in costumes. One raises a telescope and scans high,
the land beyond the houses. There's a dull shout from the
deck, and some pointing in her direction. She lifts her hand
to wave but then lets it fall. The big hats on some of them,
fussy white pants. Something flickers on a thin pole — a flag.
It quivers — bloody against the sky.

It's 9pm. The sky has cleared, and the sun has gone. A
tease of blue around the ship's dark form that now takes up
most of what used to be water. The wind has turned bitter,
and April lit the fire hours ago with wood that has flaked
over the carpet and left a sticky resin on her hands. She puts
on another log, the smoke in her hair. Her fifth cup of tea
today, and as she goes to the toilet she wonders if she should
wash herself, change her tampon. Doesn't think Andi would
notice. They've had phone sex, and they arranged to meet up
last month, but then April's sister was having an operation
— a procedure, really, but she still lay on the hospital bed,
pallid and needing April's hand. Andi was annoyed and
didn't call her for a while. A deep pit, like one dug in sand,

formed in April, and she tried to fill it with what was actually her life — laughing more liberally from behind the art shop counter; picking out new paint in ochres of yellow, orange, and brown that she got at cost price and adding them to the collection of tubes in the lounge room; making decisive marks on printouts of her thesis. She dialled his number just to hear his recorded voice on the message. The ship appeared the day she started on the big canvas, and her phone rang its guitar. Andi suggested they meet. Told her that he'd been busy, and that Sophia had been hinting at marriage, that she was ready to make a commitment.

'Do you think she's serious or is it one of her whims?' he asked. 'She's a traditional girl, deep down.'

'I don't know her.'

'You don't even believe in marriage.' Andi laughed. 'Free spirit. Remember that time in the park? I loved the way you ...' His calls are like his sex — urgent and not quite fulfilled.

Other shapes appear on the water — a fleet of them. April can't stop staring. Only a cheer from the driveway tears her away from those looming crafts to find a line of cars on the highway. Andi will never get through. She picks her way over the yard again. The patient grumble of engines that stop at her place.

'Are you open?'

April tugs the cloth off the sign and watches the cars edge into the yard, parking where they can. Others pull to the side of the road, and people get out and begin walking towards the house. At first, she asks everyone to take off their shoes at the laundry door and refuses the crumpled notes and coins. But the line grows longer until there are whole families and friend groups tromping through with dirt. They plonk their coins down on the kitchen counter until April has enough to give change for the notes.

'What do you mean you don't have EFTPOS?' an elderly person asks. 'Everyone has EFTPOS.'

They ask and ask until April gets out one of her drawing pads and slides it over with a cobalt blue pencil for email addresses — invoices she never intends to send. Someone in shorts patterned with the Southern Cross searches through the sketch pad for a spare page and makes a sign with prices: seven dollars for an adult, three dollars fifty for kids and unwaged.

When the phone rings she is digging crackers into a tub of hummus on the bench, staring out past the people who have gathered in little bunches around the tables and across the lawn, sipping water from her mugs. They face the sea, watching the way the moon's white lines eat at the ships. She isn't sure if the vessel will stop or keep moving forward when it finally reaches the shore. In the bathroom, some kids have found her condoms and blown them up as balloons, then tied them ineffectually to the cord for the blinds. One sits popped in a puddle of water left by the streaming tourists. Her phone vibrates all over the bench. Andi's voice is jolly and tense on the other end, as though she's his relative.

'Still in the city, babe. This client ... are you having a party?'

'Neighbours.'

'You should say something. How long will it take? Google says it's a theme park.'

'It's an hour if you left now. A bit longer maybe.' April

waits as Andi hisses into the phone.

'Look,' he says. His voice shows he is trying to be reasonable. April stabs at the hummus but it slips off the bench, landing upside down on the floor. 'I'll see what I can do, but it's getting a bit late now. By the time I get out there you'll probably be asleep.'

'I slept today,' she tells him, watching the dark shapes growing on the water beyond the window. There's a hoot outside and the crowd surges, waving at the ships. Andi is still talking.

'Really? Ha! Wish I could lie around all day. Yeah, look April, I'll see what I can do. Don't wear any clothes to bed and who knows? I might just surprise you. Otherwise, we'll go away somewhere soon, okay? We'll take off to Sydney and have a whole night and two days together. These next few months are going to be crazy with this client. They're taking issue with the wording. You know how they are. But after that ... God, I miss those legs of yours, those thighs ...' *Say you love them*, thinks April. But he doesn't.

The first ship has breached the bay and carved up the beach and the rise of caves. A crunching as it breaks through the ancient rock. The bow so high it covers the moon. The ship nestles in the scraggly hedges that separate the houses from the water. The crowd has formed a line, kids jiggling with excitement. April pushes past the family who have taken over the kitchen to make teas with UHT milk from deep in the pantry, white-bread-and-Vegemite sandwiches from the freezer stash. April digs around in the cupboard — pens, tubes, and frames tumble out — until she finds a piece of charcoal. Grabs the slab of smooth wood from the laundry. The first ship hasn't stopped at all but continues to plough slowly through their front yards. The deck busy with figures now, rushing around pulling at ropes that glow ghostly in the moonlight. The fancy-dress crew has vanished, leaving a sturdier lot — still clearer in April's peripheral than straight on. Tam and Lisa are out on their deck, too, sans baby. April hears them discussing which house it will go through first — most likely theirs, because even though April's place is on an angle, it's set back further from the bay. She waves to them. Inside, Andi's guitar riff starts playing. The neighbours spot her and wave back.

'No colour,' Tam calls happily.

'Sorry?' April stands on her tiptoes and leans as the ship's bow swallows their dividing fence, a giant wedge between them.

'It's no colour at all!' shouts Tam through the translucent steel. 'Ahoy, there!' Up on the deck the figures appear again. Their wigs shimmering in the cold air, red jackets with shining buttons, big old guns. Waves of dirt and sand lap up the sides. Some of the tourists break from the line.

'When does it start?' one asks April. 'Have we missed the tour?'

She is shuffled to the front. A thick rope ladder wriggles down the side of the ship. April catches it, the texture rough and sure in her hand. A pasty face frowns down from the top. He gestures impatiently. She still has the piece of wood and places her foot on the first rung uncertainly, but it's as though she was born to scale the sheer side of a pioneering ship. People below shout words of encouragement. The man in the wig nods above. And it's as though April is seeing paint for the very first time. The silver of his face and beard, the ship not just grey but battleship, slate and ash — its own painting. Halfway up she hears her phone ringing again from inside. Sharp knocking. Andi's voice through the house. There's a sucking sensation as she tries to turn away from the ship. Andi is in her house. She can see him through the windows as he pushes through the tourists into the lounge room. Tries to wave and nearly loses her grip on the railing of the ship, so hangs there on the rope, hugging the piece of wood to watch. He stops by her canvas, scowling. The cave, the colours, the style so beyond her. She turns away and finds not shame but those pulling, welcoming tones drawing her upwards. A strong calloused hand reaches over the railing to propel her to an emptiness now more ship than April. The faces of the tourists grow even paler as they clamber up behind her. No caves, no Andi, no multi-corporate clients and their diversity — everyone on the ship looks like she does against the waves of earth and house. Higher on the glowing deck, she puts charcoal to wood and starts sketching. Her point of vantage at the prow. The plants, the hills beyond. She knows the feeling of discovery. Of seeing it all for the first time. The sense that the ship will grind on through the land.

THE TWO O'CLOCK

The house we had in the country. Grandpa slept under the kitchen bench. He was pretty deaf, but on that night, there was too much noise, he said, to sleep there. He had taken his hearing aids out, which bothered us all.

'When he finally loses it,' Mum said, 'and wanders off, we won't be able to find him.'

We found him on the verandah, sleeping on the chair.

'Too much noise,' he shouted when we tried to move him.

'Grandpa's lost it,' whispered Monkey in Mum's voice.

'I heard that,' said Mum, 'it isn't pleasant.'

Grandpa's snores could already be heard from the chair.

'It's late and I'm tired,' said Mum, which is what she always said. She looked worriedly out at her dad. Pointed her matching chin at his. 'He'll be fine. It's a hot night, he'll be alright there.'

Monkey got him a pillow and I got him a quilt, and we tucked it round Grandpa's short frame. Then we picked up the hearing aids he'd left on the ground and put them in his top pocket so he wouldn't lose them. They were crusted orange with ear wax that smelled like scalp. Monkey started to write him a note, to let him know who he was and where he was and where his hearing aids were.

'Get to bed, you two,' Mum said, but tucked the almost finished note in Grandpa's small hand.

I got up to get a drink of water. It was strange not to hear Grandpa's snores coming from under the bench. To feel his breath tickle my toes. I stood near where he would normally sleep and drank my water and then I drank some more. My toes and my shins and my knees were hot, my top half cool enough. I wanted Monkey to be up so we could sing *the knee bone's connected to* together, but instead I had another glass of water, and then I needed to pee. On the way back from the toilet I decided to check on the heat that had left me when I left the kitchen. It was radiating from under the bench as though something were having a bad dream under there. I worried that Grandpa might have left his hot behind and was on the verandah, cold and frightened without it. But Grandpa was asleep, emitting a soft warmth. I tucked the note that he'd dropped back in his hand and went again to the kitchen. A little look and then back to bed.

'For it's late and I'm tired,' I whispered like Mum, and it gave me courage to crawl under the bench.

The bed for Grandpa was soft and dippy. On other nights, before the terrible hot, Monkey and I would crawl over the mattress, moving like pandas through the snow so that we wouldn't tip. When Mum was happy, she would crawl under there, too, and wait and wriggle until Grandpa returned from his night walk, and pretended that he didn't see us as he yawned and stretched and lay on his back on top of us, complaining that the lumps in his bed were getting much, much lumpier. This time I was a panda in the desert, clambering over dunes in deep white fur and getting closer and closer to the hot. It was coming from the wall, which wavered with it. And in the kitchen dark I could see the blistered paint and cracks. The wall was swelling.

Mum always came when we yelled. At any time, in any state, eating, showering, and once when we thought she'd gone away for the weekend. She rounded the corner like a football player, dipping lower so she could pluck us from the damage. It took only two yells before I saw her feet pounding and her nightie flapping. She skidded and stopped.

'Pickle?' she called fearfully.

'I'm under the bench.' I stuck my foot out to show her where.

'Get back to bed,' she said crossly. 'It's late and I'm tired.' Then she had me by the foot and there wasn't much on Grandpa's bed that I could grab on to.

'What's happening?' asked Monkey coming into the kitchen. Mum hauled me out and I saw that Monkey must have wet himself because he had no pants on.

'The wall's going to...' I thought for a moment. 'The wall's going to pop,' I announced. Mum let go of my foot and closed her eyes. 'Pickle ...' she began.

I explained about the terrible hot and the swollen wall and the paint and the cracking, but Mum looked like I was about to become a pain-in-the-arse, so I stopped.

'Is that why it's so noisy?' Monkey asked, having gone in to examine the wall and come out again.

'It's not noisy, that's just Grandpa being ...' Mum began.

'But it really is noisy,' argued Monkey bravely, 'and very hot.' We all listened hard. There was a noise, so loud it was quiet.

Mum sighed. 'Alright, but if I get in there,' she warned, getting on her knees, 'and there's nothing I'm going to become extremely cross.'

Compared to Monkey's small bum, Mum's was big. But Grandpa had told me that mine would be like that one day, so I looked elsewhere as Mum crawled under the bench. When she came out, she looked puzzled. She examined her hand and looked at the wall.

'There must be something on the other side of it,' she murmured. 'Come on, you two, let's look, and Monkey: put some pants on.' But he didn't.

The air outside was cool compared to the kitchen and the moon was bright and waxing. We filed past Grandpa, who was still snoring, into the garden and round the side of the house. First Mum, then Monkey, then me. The part of the wall in question held the rakes and the shovels and some old brooms. Mum pushed them aside and felt it, and then Monkey and I wriggled next to her and felt it, too. Cool. Mum stuck her bottom lip out and Monkey did, too. Then we trooped back to the kitchen and crouched, looking at the wall for a while. I had another glass of water. It was very hot. Mum stood abruptly and left, and we followed her. We didn't know what else to do. When we got to the verandah, she was shaking Grandpa's shoulder.

'Dad, Dad,' she said. Grandpa spluttered with his eyes

and his mouth. Monkey put his hand in Grandpa's top pocket and pulled his hearing aids out. Grandpa blinked like a goldfish. Mum turned the aids on and stuck one in a hairy ear and Grandpa's foot began to tap immediately to a hidden beat. 'There's something wrong with the wall next to your bed,' Mum said.

'Too loud,' Grandpa shouted. Mum grumbled and moved to turn the sound down on his aids.

'No, no.' Grandpa waved her hand away. 'Too loud in there.'

'Have you stuck something in the wall, Dad?'

'Mum thinks Grandpa's lost it,' Monkey whispered. Mum looked at Monkey as though he were a horrible boy and then turned back to Grandpa.

'If it's electrical, we should probably call ...' she began.

'It's late,' said Grandpa, rocking himself into a stand, 'but I'm not tired.' He peered at the watch that he never took off. 'Half one,' he announced. 'It'll really be hotting up in there.' Mum followed Grandpa into the kitchen asking questions like we did to her. The windows had begun to steam and there was a sound. A pulsing. Grandpa tapped his feet along to it. 'Can you imagine trying to sleep to this?' he yelled, getting down on his hands and knees. We crouched beside him and saw that the wall had begun to come away from the floor and a hot red light shone from beneath it.

'What is it?' I breathed into the red and the heat and the pulsing.

'It's the two o'clock,' Grandpa answered. He looked surprised that I should ask. Mum gaped nervously at the wall pushing away from the floor. And at the red light that shone on Grandpa's bed. 'What do you reckon, my girl?' Grandpa

asked her. 'Shall we take a look?' Mum stared at him a
moment and then, as though her brain went flop, something
seemed to slip away. It was late and we could see that
Mum was very tired. She nodded vaguely and disappeared,
coming back with a crowbar. 'You'll need to jimmy the wall
away from the floor,' Grandpa instructed. 'It should fall
away easily.' Mum crawled slowly and hesitantly under the
bench. Grandpa smacked Monkey's bare bum. 'You go put
some pants on. They don't like that sort of thing in there
and don't you own a dress?' he asked me. I did have one. I
used it for dress-ups. Monkey and I slid to the bedroom and
found pants for him and the dress for me. I couldn't do the
zipper up and worried, as we went back down the hall, that
Grandpa would think it wasn't suitable.

There was an enormous *riiiiip*, and we ran to the kitchen
to see the wall crumbling slowly away. Mum stood near
with her mouth ajar, the crowbar dangling from her hand.
I wanted to tell Monkey that Mum looked like an action
figure, but the hot red light had filled the room. Where the
bench had been was a hall — bigger than the one in town
— with decorations hanging from the roof and a slippery
wooden floor filled with people sliding and shuffling in big
dresses and shoes so shiny that when the dust had settled,
we could see up the skirts. No one noticed the wall or our
kitchen or the four of us staring. Clicking his fingers and
tapping his feet against bits of plaster and paint, Grandpa
picked his way over the rubble. Mum might have been
calling, *Dad, Dad*, but Grandpa had pulled his hearing aids
out and tossed them on the ground. Anyway, no one could
hear her over the band. She looked at us as though we might
have answers. We shrugged. So Mum gripped my hand, and

I gripped Monkey's hand, and we stumbled over the debris into the big red room. In the shiny hall, the shiny people in dresses and shiny shoes danced faster and faster.

'Anytime now,' Grandpa yelled appearing beside us. 'It'll be two any moment.' He looked excited and new. A lady with nice cheeks and familiar eyes pulled at his arm and Grandpa disappeared into the crowd. If we'd known that would be the last time we saw him, we might have given him a hug. As it was, someone else had asked Mum to dance, and she beamed and tugged at her nightie and warned us over her shoulder to keep together and not get lost. Monkey and I danced together. He didn't seem to mind my dress, and when he stood with his toes on mine, we could almost keep up with the whirling crowd. We danced like that to three whole songs. Then the floor shook with a gonging almost as loud as the terrible hot had been burning. People spun and fluttered. They pointed to a big clock on the wall. Two o'clock.

The dance was like any other — with feet moves and hand moves and hip moves. But there were face moves, too. And no one did the same move as anyone else in time. The music was so fast that there was no beat — just a slanting and a ratta-tat-tat rhythm that shook the walls and made them move so that everyone was juggled in closer together. Some people hopped. Some jigged. Some shook their hair, so all their lovely curls came out. Some rolled around on the floor. Monkey and I clung to the moving walls and watched. We saw Mum using one foot to propel herself and her partner round and round and round. We thought we saw Grandpa doing the chicken dance. Once we'd decided that you could do anything at all at the two o'clock, we thought we'd be polar bears on ice and skidded and slid around the shiny

floor, roaring and bumping into legs and feet. We saw other
animals there. Some pigs with lipstick on their snouts. And
some very happy-looking emus who used their bums to
knock one another over. The two o'clock lasted for such a
long time that the walls ran with water. People collapsed on
one another, helplessly. The band broke all their instruments
until it was just the horn player, puffing and puffing until
his cheeks became see-through and his horn had to be
taken away. Then it was quieter, with just some oinking and
giggling and sighing as everyone tried to collect themselves
and their partners — brushing the sweat from everything
they owned. They got up slowly from the floor and hugged
and danced around a little more in the hot quiet. The man
with Mum gave her a folded note and smiled her a special
smile and didn't seem to mind at all about her nightie. Mum
and Monkey and I watched him fade into a curtain by the
stage.

Although we waited near the wall until well after the
place had emptied and the big red lights had been turned
off, Grandpa never came. We climbed back through and
searched the cold house.

'He must have gone to sleep on the verandah,' Mum said.
But he wasn't there. Back in the kitchen, the wall had rebuilt
itself. The bench was where it usually was and Grandpa's bed
was underneath it, soft and dipped, but empty. Mum sat on
the edge of his bed and slowly opened the note that the man
had given her. Monkey and I watched with our heads on her
shoulders. We knew that notes often had love messages on
them. But Mum was hoping for a phone number so that she

could call the man up and ask about Grandpa. The paper was thin with blue lines that faded towards the middle. We used the same sort for shopping. *YOU ARE GRANDPA*, the note said in big letters that found it hard to keep to the lines. *YOU ARE ON THE VERANDAH AT HOME. YOUR HEARING AIDS ARE IN YOUR TOP POCKET AND THE* ... Monkey's handwriting petered off. Mum closed her eyes. And we all lay down on Grandpa's bed under the bench.

KING

My eyes fail. They had me by the ear before I knew where I was. I was by the old house. The roof had caved, but there was food all around and more on the way. You could smell it. I had a feed, then got to staring. Thinking about hunger. There's no use thinking about hunger. You're either hungry or you're not and I'm not, but the food went to my gut, and I guess I'd got to staring when they grabbed me by the ear in the dark. They use teeth, the bastards. I could hardly see, but I knew there were two. One doing the ripping and the other sort of dancing and laughing. My head cleared when the blood let. Pain can do that. I thought, don't go for that one with the teeth — he's tasted blood, he's clear — go for the kid. So I went for the kid, kicked the hell out of him — kicked him in the face and in the back, and when I'd finished, I could see a hole in his side and could hear him. He wasn't laughing. I'd got it right.

That was the kid and here was the dad ready to go but clouded up like a dam. My kid got killed years back. I couldn't help her. The mother wouldn't leave. We have to go,

I told her, but she wouldn't leave, her eyes were like clouds. God knows where she is now. He let go of me with a bit of my ear in his mouth, which he swallowed before he leaned to come in for the kill and that's when I got him. Took his eye and half his face and out of the holes came this screaming. They got away through the trees. I could hear him screaming along the track with his son whimpering behind, all through the bushes and down towards the water. There was nothing I could do for them. My ear was off and there was no one to clean it. No water, no lover, just night.

At dawn my face was hard with blood. My ear hurt like hell, and there was a dull, deep pain through my body. I was stiff with it. It had been a cold night. I wanted a drink. My head exploded with every movement. I heard something move with my good ear and I stopped, listened; it was nothing. Then I'd move and hear it shadowing me. I thought it might be them, but they'd be dead by now, or looked after. That one with the teeth is the sort who's got it all and wants more. I know him, he's me. But not anymore.

When you're in the state I'm in, the local waterhole is a good and a bad place to go. On the one hand, you can get a drink. Except for the really dry times when everyone's about to rip each other apart, you can pretty much always get a drink. On the other, it's noisy. So damned noisy that if trouble comes, you're likely not to hear it, won't know it until it's on top of you or got a piece of you in its teeth. I went down and saw others, but I stayed on my side, took a few drinks, and looked around. Drank again. I was nervous. I didn't stay too long. I'm old now. It's not like before.

•

Halfway up the hill I knew I couldn't go back to the house. It had been lucky for me but now it wasn't. If those bastards didn't come, others would — they smell hurt. And fear. Treacherous smells. They'd try it again in the night. Then again, I couldn't go back. Before, I always knew where I was. Chasing tail, mostly. I'd make the approach, muscle up a bit, see if she wanted some — they were always playing it coy, making you chase half the day before they decided, and, in the meantime, there were other bastards sniffing around. I used to pull myself right up until they were forced to crouch, and the lady would look at them and look at me and make her decision. You had to laugh. But if she took too long or if some dickhead put me off my game, there was always another. And another. Some of them had a kid. Some of the kids were mine. Sometimes one of the others would slip one in and there'd be kids by him, too. Didn't matter. I'd just wait until they grew up, show them a thing or two.

And he was one of those kids. Not mine but someone else's, some big fucker, almost as big as me, but he couldn't fight and would just dig a pit and lay around waiting. I guess he waited long enough one day. She was older — she'd seen kids come and go — but I never managed to breed with her. You had to admire that big patient bastard. And where was he now? Dead? Who cares? He did his job. That son of his made me what I am today. Hardly nothing.

I came to a hill with thin trees all around. It was day, but darkening. Before long, the rain came, thundered down, and those trees hardly stopped it. It rained all over me. I could feel it in my ear, in the holes in my face, in my eyes, how the tacky blood came unstuck and ran into the ground. When it slowed to a drizzle, I moved my face and the holes felt clean. Didn't stink so much of blood. The sun came and lit everything with silver sparks. I moved along slow, drenched but easy, meeting no one.

When the air dried, every little twerp was out in it. I could hardly hear with my good ear for the racket. Nothing to drink and still the noise. I stumbled through the narrow lanes and tunnels, the sudden dips, logs, and went for the open. I knew a place. Everything else in me was shot, but my nose worked fine. Right through the gradual clearing of things, the way the light worked stronger and stronger as you got out of the throng. That fence, a gate with holes in it from the years of climbing through. It was familiar, right to my gut. I paced the wire, worried I'd misjudge it and be stuck — strung up and waiting for the bastards to take me away in bits. But it was the place alright. I could smell the food. It smelled like home to me. I crawled under, like some kid, and my old heart gave a giddy jump. Hell, I even leapt towards that green, towards a time when I was the one they all crouched for. I remembered.

They say you won't remember. But I did. It was in the body. It was in the ache. It was all through me. I could smell them. They were still there. It was spring, and you know spring — everyone's up for it, guzzling their body weight before all the drink dries up, gone again. A few dry times ago there was a fire and you could hear the screaming. Everyone was screaming. I smelled it in the distance — things weren't so bad for me then. He'd got me, but I was new to it and pretty much excited about being on my own. Then I smelled the fear, and I heard the fear, and I saw the fear coming down like hot orange rain. Over the ridge the sky was filled with screaming, and then the sky was filled with a silence I never want to hear again.

I guess I'd got to staring and then he was in front of me on the hill. A mother fucking mountain. That big bastard's son, bigger than any I've seen, and young, too, stock still. Every bit coiled. I remembered how that could be. Down the bottom of the hill the dam shone in the sun and next to it, his mob, staring. I couldn't see his mother — there'd been tough times I suppose. I *smelled* the others. I wanted them again, but doubted they'd have had much use for me. It didn't matter. Something about being old makes you an idiot. I should have crouched low, coughed politely. Twice. It's the done thing. Instead, I moved closer. He didn't remember me, just thought I was some crazy old bastard wandered from his mob.

He kept his stance. I thought, *I should move on*. But I wanted him to know me. Despite the beating he'd given me back then, despite being the rogue, I was still kicking. I rose up. Christ, my body hurt. I went up slow, climbing the air. Saw him jolt. He *moved*. He was surprised to see me. I guess I might've been a thing to see: ear gone, hair matted from the rain, skinny, fat, old and half gone. And something else he saw in me. That, or he hadn't stuck it with any of the females for a while and wanted to prove himself. He bent to rub on the tall stalks of grass, dipping again and again and getting them good and drenched with his smell. Once he'd finished perfuming the whole damned paddock, he pulled up high — you could stretch your neck getting a look at the bastard. I was half dead already from all the stretching, but I found something — maybe the thing he could see, and I couldn't — and got myself a little higher. Then he came at me.

What's it like to fight? Well you don't use your teeth, that's a sly bastard's game. Once you get past teeth with them there's nothing, just soft flesh and whingeing. No, the power's in the hind. A kick from me or him that could fuck you till Friday. Beyond Friday. Forever and a day. He gave me something like that years back, when I was King and he decided it was his turn for a run. I came along trying to get a whiff of his mother. She just went on and on being wantable. I liked breeding with older females. The older they got the more often they bred boys, and the boys would grow up and try to take me on. That made me laugh, it did. Instead of her I found him with no politeness, no coughing or crouching. Just grown and waiting. Now he went in, chest first like a kid, and that was unusual so I stumbled, maybe that was his game. He swiped my nose — just a nick, a warning, but I bled — then he got me in a hug, and we fell backwards.

I regained my ground, and I went in at him in that same childish way and came to enjoy it, like I was a kid, too. But he'd had enough of games. He pulled back to square up. Jumped forward, balanced back, could've gone in for the kill, but again he waited. I didn't trust my balance anymore and that's a sure sign that death day is near. Thinking like this made me want to laugh, lie on the grass, and complain that my springs were rusty. Tell him about times when there was nothing to drink and times when there was too much. Tell him about the fire. But his mob was behind him. Behind me there was only the bush. The night. From the nothingness I found my strength.

We balanced and kicked. He was getting in most of the blows. He slashed my shoulder and gave a thump to the good side of my head so there was ringing, then silence, and all I knew was the kicking and the immense bloody smell of him — the scent of a King. He was giving me a pounding alright, slowly tearing me to shreds, but there was no kill. It was a dangerous game he was playing — if I was fitter, younger, if I had anything more than old bones to give, I might have got the upper hand. That big bastard who squired him hadn't taught him how you could get the upper hand.

I wanted to show him how the real game starts. Yeah, you stuff around for a while, young'un, but then you smell it, that whiff of final blood and you go in for the kill. I could smell it. It was coming from me. I balanced back, *here's how you do it kid*, back, *here's how you let it go*, shot out with a kick that could change time, *here's how you bring it down*, slashed from his chest to his crotch, *here's how you bring it home*, and pulled. Everything in him came out. He staggered, then collapsed. Alarm rippled through the mob, but they stayed still. Perfectly. He gave a final hack. Died. His blood blackened the ground.

I was King. My arm hung and the hole where my ear used to be bled into my eye. I was King. I shuffled towards the mob. Half blind. Deaf. King. A few of the males edged forward. If they crouched, they did so only with a slight dip. I couldn't hear the coughing. They scratched their chests. One little bastard bent only to rub his scent on a long stalk of grass. They were readying. They'd come for me. One by one. If not today, then tomorrow. And if not tomorrow ... I could hear the death coming like rain. Like fire.

ACKNOWLEDGEMENTS

This collection wouldn't have been possible without the tremendous generosity of Fiona Stager and Kevin Guy, and the team at Avid Reader Bookshop, in sharing the writers' room — space that has allowed me to bring these stories together. An Australia Council for the Arts Grant has been fundamental to the development of this project. Marika Webb-Pullman's vision for these stories has brought such joy and strength to the writing and editing process — she is the rarest and wisest of publishers.

The publishing team at Scribe have worked tirelessly on this collection. A phone call from Cora Roberts is always the most exciting. So much admiration and thanks to Molly Slight, Adam Howard, and the team at Scribe UK as well as to Emily Cook at Scribe US. Also to Henry Rosenbloom, Tace Kelly, Laura Thomas, and Alice Richardson, along with the Scribe family who endlessly champion their authors.

There have been many editors, readers, and advisers on these stories over the years — special thanks to Tom Doig, Anne Whisken, and Hayden Whisken. To Brea Acton,

Romy Ash, Kelly Chandler, Laura Elvery, Henry Feltham, Michelle Ferris, Veronica Gorrie, Robert Harding, Ingrid Horrocks, Kris Kneen, Anna Krien, Lisa Lang, Bella Li, Nic Low, Tina Makereti, Mirandi Riwoe, Josephine Rowe, Amy Spiers, Jim Thompson-Martin, and countless others — thank you!

These stories were written over two decades and through support from residencies and funding bodies. Thank you to (in roughly chronological order) the Dunmoochin Foundation, the Asialink Literature Residency, Rosebank Retreat, Laughing Waters Residency, Booranga Writers' Centre, The Territory Wildlife Park Artists Residency, The Martin Bequest Travelling Scholarship, The Stella Prize, The Wheeler Centre Hot Desk, and The Victorian Premier's Literature Award. Thank you for the space and support of the Rosalind Price beach house residency, the Jenny Gill, Harry Doig, Mary Slater, and Andrew Watson beach house residency, The Jack Doig and Jeanne-Marie Cole chambre de bonne residency, and the ongoing Anne and Hayden Whisken family residency! My warm thanks to the University of Melbourne Creative Writing department, in particular Dr Dominique Hecq, Dr Amanda Johnson, and Professor Kevin Brophy; to my colleagues at Massey University; to the writing community of Aotearoa; and to the Australasian Animal Studies Association.

Thank you to the more-than-human world. Especially, for this collection: working dogs; the cows living through the Number One Dairy Unit in Palmerston North; the crocodiles of the Northern Territory; and, always, the mosquito.

Versions, extracts, and lines from these stories have previously been published in *A Kind of Shelter*

– *Whakaruru-taha*, *Best Australian Stories*, *The Big Issue*, *Cordite*, *Etchings*, *Hecate*, *J Journal*, *Newsroom*, *The North American Review*, *The Saturday Paper*, *Sleepers Almanac*, *Penguin Plays Rough*, *Poetry of Encounter*, *Vice*, and *The Victorian Writer*. 'Those Last Days of Summer' was published in *Co-respond* in response to Jade Burstall's artwork 'Trading Futures'. I am grateful to the editors of these journals and collections for their support in accepting or commissioning this early work.

Most of all, thank you to my darling, Tom Doig, for sharing this big life with me, for telling me to write another story collection, and for seeing this — and all of our words and world — through.